P9-DGR-293

ALL BUT ALICE

ALL BUT ALICE

Phyllis Reynolds Naylor

A Jean Karl Book
Atheneum 1992 New York

Maxwell Macmillan Canada
Toronto

Maxwell Macmillan International
New York Oxford Singapore Sydney

Atheneum
Macmillan Publishing Company
866 Third Avenue
New York, NY   10022

Maxwell Macmillan Canada, Inc.
1200 Eglinton Avenue East
Suite 200
Don Mills, Ontario M3C 3N1

Macmillan Publishing Company is part of the Maxwell Communication
Group of Companies.

First edition
Printed in the United States of America
10 9 8 7 6 5 4 3 2 1
The text of this book is set in 12 pt. Cheltenham

Library of Congress Cataloging-in-Publication Data
Naylor, Phyllis Reynolds.
All but Alice/Phyllis Reynolds Naylor. —1st ed.
    p.   cm.
"A Jean Karl book."
Summary: Seventh-grader Alice decides that the only way to stave off
personal and social disasters is to be part of the crowd, especially the "in"
crowd, no matter how boring and, potentially, difficult.
ISBN 0–689–31773–5
[1. Conduct of life—Fiction. 2. Clubs—Fiction. 3. Interpersonal relations—
Fiction. 4. Schools—Fiction.]
I. Title.
PZ7.N24Alm   1992
[Fic]—dc20   91–28722

*To Laura and Rachel,
the newest members of our family,
with love*

Contents

One   Keepsakes   1
Two   A Major Operation   9
Three   Losing Loretta   21
Four   Zombie Girls   33
Five   Sex   45
Six   Friends   57
Seven   The Earring Club   68
Eight   Mar-i-lyn   78
Nine   Mayday   83
Ten   Modern Love   95
Eleven   Wonder Woman   106
Twelve   Snow   115
Thirteen   In Between   127
Fourteen   The Test   135
Fifteen   All but Alice   142

1

Keepsakes

WHAT I'VE decided about life is this: If you don't have a mother, you need a sister. And if you don't have a sister, you need a bulletin board.

Elizabeth Price, across the street, has a room with twin beds, with white eyelet bedspreads on each, a little dressing table and stool, a lamp with a white eyelet ruffle for a shade, and a bulletin board covered with photos of Elizabeth in her ballet costume, her tap shoes and pants, her gymnastic leotards, and her Camp Fire Girl uniform, which isn't too surprising, since there's a huge photograph over the couch in their living room of Elizabeth in her first communion dress.

Pamela Jones, down the next block, has pictures of movie stars and singers on hers. She also has a dried rose, which Mark Stedmeister gave her once, an autograph by Madonna, a pom-pom, which her cousin in New Jersey sent her, and a photograph of her and Mark, taken from behind, with their arms around each other and their hands in each other's hip pockets.

I'd seen those bulletin boards dozens of times when I stayed overnight at Pamela's or Elizabeth's, but suddenly, in the winter of seventh grade, I wanted one of my own more than anything else I could think of.

What I wanted was to know I was growing up normally—that I was in step with every female person in Montgomery County, that I was a part of the great sisterhood of women. I wanted to see the highlights of *my* life pinned up on the wall. I wanted to make sure I *had* a life.

"I'd like a bulletin board for my room," I told Dad one night when he was cleaning the broiler. "Pamela and Elizabeth both have one, and I want a place where I can pin up things."

"I've got an extra one at the store. I'll try to remember to bring it home," he said.

I get a lot of weird things that way. Dad is manager of the Melody Inn, one of a chain of music stores, so he can bring home whatever he wants. Usually it's stuff that's defective or doesn't sell; so far I've got two posters of Prince; one of Mozart; a couple of slightly warped drumsticks, which I gave to Patrick, who used to be my boyfriend; a Beethoven bikini from the Melody Inn Gift Shoppe, which says, HAPPY BIRTHDAY, BEETHOVEN, on the seat of the pants, only the print is crooked; and some notepads, with CHOPIN-LISZT printed at the top.

The following afternoon, there was a huge bulletin board, a little dusty, with one corner chipped, hanging on the wall above my bureau.

"It's great!" I told Dad. "Aunt Sally used to have a bulletin board in her kitchen, didn't she? I remember she used to pin up pictures I drew in kindergarten."

"That was your *mother*, Al." (My name is Alice McKinley—Alice Kathleen McKinley, to be exact—but Dad and Lester call me Al.) "And those were pictures you'd made in nursery school. Don't you remember how your mother kept photos of you and Lester on it too?"

I always manage to do that. Mom died when I was five—four or five, I can't remember which—and I always seem to mix her up with Aunt Sally, who took care of us for a while afterward.

"Yeah, I think I do," I told Dad, but I wasn't really sure.

I set aside the whole evening to work on my bulletin board, and took a box of keepsakes from my closet to see what was worth pinning up—something as wonderful as an autograph by Madonna or a photo of me in a ballet costume. Carefully I scooped things out of the box and spread them around on my bed.

There was an envelope, yellow around the edges. I looked inside: grass. A handful of dry grass. And then I remembered Donald Sheavers back in fourth grade, when we lived in Takoma Park. We were playing

Tarzan out in the backyard, and we had a big piece of cardboard for a raft. At some point he was supposed to kiss me, but every time he tried, I got the giggles and rolled off. For a whole afternoon Donald tried to kiss me, and though I wanted him to, it was just too embarrassing. So after he went home, I pulled up a handful of grass from under the cardboard to remember him by.

Stuffing the grass back into the envelope, I picked up a tag off my first pair of Levi's. I'd been wearing Sears Toughskins through most of elementary, and when I got to sixth grade, Lester had taken me to buy some real Levi's. I studied the label now in my hand and tried to imagine Pamela and Elizabeth looking at it in admiration and awe. I put the label on top of the grass.

I couldn't figure out what the next thing was. When I unrolled it, I saw that it was a piece of brown wrapping paper with leaves drawn on it. And then I remembered the sixth-grade play, where Pamela had the lead role—the part I'd wanted—and I had to be a bramble bush instead. I put the brown wrapping paper over by the Levi's label and the grass. It was very discouraging.

Then I felt that sort of thump in the chest you get when you come across something important, and I picked up an envelope with ALICE M. on the front, decorated with drawings of hearts, and airplanes with red stripes on the wings.

Inside was one of those misty-looking photographs of a man and woman walking through the woods holding hands, and you can't see their faces. At the top, in curly letters, were the words A SPECIAL FEELING WHEN I THINK OF YOU. There weren't any printed words when you opened it up, but someone had written in blue ink, "I like you a lot." A valentine from Patrick from sixth grade! I decided I'd put the card up on my bulletin board but not the envelope. I could never explain the airplanes to Pamela and Elizabeth, because I couldn't understand them myself.

What was left in the box was the wrapper of a 3 Musketeers bar that Patrick had given me; the stub of a train ticket when I'd gone to Chicago to visit Aunt Sally; a ring from my favorite teacher, Mrs. Plotkin; a book of matches from Patrick's country club; and a program from the *Messiah* sing-along that I had gone to last Christmas, with Dad and my language arts teacher.

This was it! This was my life! I turned the box upside down again and shook it hard to see if an autograph from Michael Jackson or something might fall out, but all I got was a dead moth.

I took thumbtacks and put up the valentine from Patrick, the train ticket stub, Mrs. Plotkin's ring tied to a ribbon, the matchbook, and the program from the *Messiah*. They hardly filled up one corner.

I clomped downstairs for the Ritz crackers, but Lester had them. He was sitting at the kitchen table over a copy of *Rolling Stone*.

Dad was drinking some ginger ale. "How's the bulletin board coming?" he asked.

"I think it's too big," I mumbled, flopping down on

a chair. "I haven't had enough great moments in my life, I guess."

"Well, think about the ones you *have* had, and see if you can't come up with something," he told me.

"My first bra, my first pair of Levi's," I said. "I suppose I *could* put the labels up, but there's still three-fourths of the board yet to go."

Lester put a squirt of Cheez Whiz on a cracker and popped it in his mouth. "You could hang your whole bra and jeans on the bulletin board and then you wouldn't have any space left at all," he said.

I gave him a look. Lester's only twenty, but he's got a mustache, and girls go crazy over him. Don't ask me why, but they do. Right at that very moment he had a blob of Cheez Whiz in his mustache.

"Keep thinking," I told him.

"Remember when Patrick took you to the country club?" Lester said. "When you got home, you discovered you'd stuffed one of their cloth napkins in your purse. That'd be good for a twelve-inch square of space."

I was desperate. "I can't have Pamela and Elizabeth over just to see a label off my jeans and a train ticket! I've hardly got anything at all." I threw back my head and wailed: "My life is a blank bulletin board!"

Lester put down his magazine. "Al," he said, "what you do is you take off all your clothes, drag your bulletin board out in the street, and take an ax to it. By tomorrow morning, you'll have a policeman's jacket, a hospital ID bracelet, and a newspaper story to add to your collection. Maybe even a photograph of you in the policeman's jacket, climbing into the back of a paddy wagon. I guarantee it."

I stomped back upstairs and sat glaring at the near-empty bulletin board. Chances were, in another year, I wouldn't even want some of the things that were up there now!

And then it came to me that I would probably have this bulletin board until I was through college. I was twelve, and if I graduated when I was twenty-one, that was nine more years. It wasn't as though my life was over. It was still being written, and the thing about bulletin boards—the *reason* for bulletin boards—was you could change things around. Add and subtract. Then I didn't feel so bad.

The phone rang. It was Pamela.

"Guess what?" she said breathlessly.

"You got a newer, bigger bulletin board," I guessed.

"No. Mother said I can start wearing different earrings now, Alice! I don't have to go on wearing these little gold balls I've had since third grade. I can wear *wires* if I want. Even loops! You want to go shopping with us this weekend?"

I knew right then I could not go another year, another month, another week even, without pierced ears. Whatever Pamela did, that's what I'd do. Whatever Elizabeth had, that's what I wanted. Always before, Dad and I smiled secretly at the kids who came in the music store all dressed alike, all wearing black, all with an earring in one ear and the same kind of makeup. I'd think how stupid it was to try to be a copy of someone else.

But suddenly it was happening to me. I was turning into a lemming! If all the girls in junior high suddenly raced to the roof and plunged madly over the edge, I would be sailing off into space with them.

2

A Major Operation

I WAITED till breakfast the next morning to spring it on
Dad. Lester always moves through breakfast in a fog
(he eats cold leftovers because he can't trust himself
to aim a carton of milk over some cornflakes), but Dad
is at his best in the mornings.

At the exact moment he had drunk a little coffee
but hadn't started the newspaper, I said, "Do you realize I'm the only seventh-grade girl in the state of
Maryland who doesn't have pierced ears?" I decided I
might as well paint the big picture while I was at it.

Dad just smiled and reached for the butter. "I didn't
know you had so many friends."

"Dad . . . !"

We were distracted right then by Lester, who had
just slung a saucer of leftover chicken and noodles on

the table, and was fumbling around, trying to find the chair. I can't figure out why Les doesn't shave and wash first and *then* come to breakfast, but he says if he shaved in his sleep he'd probably cut off his nose.

"There's plastic wrap on that chicken, Les," Dad reminded him. I tried not to look as Lester picked up a blob of congealed noodles. He chewed with his head resting on one hand.

"Seriously, Dad," I said, "I can't think of one other girl—well, maybe one, one or two—in seventh grade who doesn't have her ears pierced. I mean, you're just not *with* it unless you wear earrings."

"Your mother wore earrings, and she never had her ears pierced," Dad said.

"Those were clip earrings, Dad, and they hurt. All the best ones, the *pretty* ones, are for pierced ears. *Please!* I can pay for it myself."

Dad spread butter on his toast, took another sip of coffee, unfolded the newspaper, and just when I thought he wasn't going to answer at all, he said, "When it comes to doing something permanent to your body, Al, I just don't know. . . ."

"It's not a tattoo on my forehead! It's not a nose job! All I want is a little microscopic hole in each earlobe. *Please!*"

"If that's all there is to it, why are you asking me?"

"Because I have to have a parent's signature," I confessed.

"I had a teacher once who had pierced ears," said Lester, warming to the conversation. "Her earlobes were so stretched that you could see light through the holes."

I didn't even look at him, just kept my eyes on Dad, like a Labrador retriever watching his master.

"I don't want you doing something you'll regret later," Dad went on. "I don't know a thing about pierced ears."

Lester began to sing some stupid song he'd learned in Cub Scouts:

"Do your ears hang low?
Do they wobble to and fro?
Can you tie them in a knot?
Can you tie them in a bow?
Can you sling them over your shoulder
Like a Continental soldier?
Do your ears—hang—low?"

I almost bawled.

"Tell you what," said Dad. "Talk it over with some-one we trust—a grown-up someone, I mean—and if she gives the go-ahead, then it's okay with me."

I reached across the table and hugged him.

My first thought was of Lester's ex-girlfriends, Mar-ilyn and Crystal, but since neither had spoken to him since Christmas, I didn't think it was wise to bring them back in the picture again. Janice Sherman, the assistant manager at the Melody Inn, didn't have pierced ears. Loretta Jenkins, who ran the Gift Shoppe, did, but hers were pierced in two places, and I could guarantee that whatever Loretta Jenkins of the Wild Hair said, Dad wouldn't pay one bit of attention to.

"Call Aunt Sally," Dad suggested.

"*Not* Aunt *Sally!*"

"Call Carol," said Les, the first intelligent thing he'd said since he came to the table. Carol is Aunt Sally's daughter, but you'd never know it.

Dad nodded. "I'd trust Carol. Whatever she says goes."

I ran upstairs to brush my teeth, then charged out the door with my book bag to tell Elizabeth and Pamela.

There was slush on the sidewalks, which is what you get most of in Maryland in January, and it splashed over the tops of my sneakers. Pamela was at the bus stop already, telling Elizabeth about how she was going to start out with wire earrings and end up with all the exotic things you see in the department stores.

When I walked up, the smile on my face stretching halfway to China, Pamela paused in midsentence: "What's with *you?*"

I couldn't stop grinning. "I get to have my ears pierced," I said, and Pamela squealed like a runt pig.

We both looked at Elizabeth. "Why don't you have your ears done too?" Pamela asked. "Then the three of us could shop together."

Elizabeth hugged her books to her chest. "I don't think I could stand it."

"It's not bad, Elizabeth, really!" Pamela promised. "You hardly even feel it. Just a quick pinch."

"It's not that. . . ."

"*What,* then?" I asked.

Elizabeth shifted uncomfortably, "I just . . . I just can't stand the thought of holes."

"But they're only tiny pinpricks," said Pamela.

"I don't care."

"They heal right up if you take care of them."

Elizabeth shook her head.

"It's not as though they're the only holes in your body," I said. "Your ears are holes. Your nostrils are holes. Your . . ."

"Don't *talk* about it!" said Elizabeth.

The bus came and we got on. Pamela slid onto a seat beside some boy just because he said "Hi," so I sat by Elizabeth. I guess when you have blond hair so long you can sit on it, like Pamela does, you can sit with almost any boy you want.

"I can see it coming," Elizabeth said miserably. "If *you* get your ears pierced, I'll be the only girl left who doesn't wear earrings. If I'm ever interviewed for the school newspaper, the reporter will write, 'Elizabeth Price, the girl with the virgin earlobes.' "

I'd never even heard Elizabeth say the word *virgin* before. "They're your ears," I said. "You can do whatever you want."

Elizabeth sighed and slumped down in the seat. "You know what I hate, Alice? Bodies."

"That's too bad," I told her, seeing as how she was stuck with one for life.

"I could be perfectly happy if I was just a mind and a soul. Do you ever think about things like that?"

"No," I told her. "I think about whether you were dropped on your head as a baby, Elizabeth. Sometimes I really do." I wasn't very understanding of Elizabeth that day, but she wanted to talk soul and I wanted to talk earrings.

That evening, as soon as dinner was over, I dialed my cousin Carol in Chicago. Suddenly things were starting to happen in my life. Only a day or so ago, I'd been thinking bulletin boards, and now I was thinking pierced ears. What would I be thinking about the day after tomorrow? Being twelve, almost thirteen, meant all kinds of wonderful surprises coming my way, and I imagined how Carol would welcome me to the fold of pierced ears. Then I heard the phone stop ringing and someone saying, "Yes?" Aunt Sally!

I tried to disguise my voice and spoke as low as it would go. "May I speak with Carol, please?"

"Alice McKinley with a cold!" Aunt Sally declared. "You haven't been outside without a jacket, have you?"

"I'm fine," I said. "I just had a frog in my throat for a moment. What are you doing in Carol's apartment?"

"Cleaning," replied Aunt Sally.

"Is Carol there?"

"No, she flew to Florida with a girlfriend," Aunt Sally told me. "She decided to take a few vacation days to lie on the beach and get herself a melanoma."

Talking with Aunt Sally is like playing Russian roulette. You never know what's coming at you next. I didn't know what to do. I certainly didn't want to wait until Carol got back from Florida, in case Dad changed his mind.

"Is there anything *I* can do for you, dear?" Aunt Sally wanted to know.

"Uh . . . I don't think so," I told her.

"Try me," she said.

"Well . . . I just . . . we were talking . . . I was thinking . . . does Carol have pierced ears, Aunt Sally?"

"Against my better judgment, yes, she does."

"Well, I want to get mine done, and—"

"Oh, Alice! Those sweet little ears you were born with?"

"Well, I haven't traded them in or anything."

"What would your mother say?"

"Listen, Aunt Sally, almost every girl in seventh grade has her ears pierced, and Dad says its okay with him as long as I get some advice."

Advice was the wrong word. Saying *advice* to Aunt Sally is like saying *mush* to an Alaskan husky.

"Well, dear, I'll tell you everything I know," Aunt Sally said. "When Carol came home after her ears were pierced, they were fiery red. I mean, these are *puncture* wounds we're talking about, and you have to marinate your ears in rubbing alcohol for two months to keep from getting gangrene. Carol hardly slept at all the first night. You can't take the earrings out, you know. Once you get your ears pierced, you have to leave something in them at all times, and—"

"Well, thanks a lot, Aunt Sally," I said, signing off.

"Just a minute, Alice. I can tell that nothing I say is going to stop you, so remember just one thing: septicemia."

"What?"

"Blood poisoning. If you go to one of those fly-by-night places, and they use unsterilized needles, you could be dead within twenty-four hours and not even know it. All for those little dangly things to wear in your ears."

I swallowed.

"If you *are* determined to get your ears pierced, call a reputable jewelry store and make an appointment. They hire registered nurses, Carol said, to come in and do the piercing. Don't go to one of those little booths at a mall."

"Okay, Aunt Sally!" I told her.

"Just do one thing for me, Alice, and let it be the guide for the rest of your life: Ask yourself whether your mother would be more or less proud of you if you did whatever you're thinking of doing."

"I'll remember. Thanks a lot," I said, and hung up.

I let my back slide down the wall, my feet slipping out in front of me, until I was sitting on the floor, the telephone in my lap. How did *I* know what my mother would think about it? I hardly even remembered my mother. But the more I thought, the more I imagined her saying, "Alice, it doesn't make one bit of difference to me." That's what I hoped she'd say, anyway. So I looked up jewelry stores in the yellow pages, dialed one, and made an appointment for Friday evening. I felt like a grown-up already.

I called Pamela, and we squealed back and forth over the telephone like mice. Her mother said she could take us downtown Friday evening, and for the rest of the week, the girls at school gave me little bits of advice.

"For the first five days, you'll feel like your ears have a fever."

"Get little gold balls and you won't have so much trouble sleeping. Don't get studs that are pointed or anything."

"Use hydrogen peroxide instead of rubbing alcohol and it won't dry your skin."

"Turn them at least once a day."

Friday came and I was up an hour early. I washed my ears extra well so they'd be presentable for the nurse at the jewelry store, and was already at the table when Dad and Lester came down to breakfast.

"Puncture Day, huh?" said Lester, groping for the refrigerator.

"Jealous?" I asked him.

"Get real," he said.

But Pamela wasn't at the bus stop that morning, and she didn't come to school later. As soon as I got home that afternoon, I phoned.

"Oh, Alice," said her mother. "We've all got the flu. We'll simply have to make that appointment for some other time. I'm sorry."

I stood in the hallway, arms dangling. I *had* to get my ears pierced that day. It would be weeks, the girls told me, before I could wear any earrings I wanted. I was willing to go the rest of January with nothing but gold studs in my earlobes, but then I wanted little porcelain cats, little silver stars, loops, dangles, tiny purple flowers. If I didn't get them pierced today, Aunt Sally would send us a clipping about how pierced ears caused brain cancer.

I couldn't call Dad and ask him to take off work, because the Melody Inn is open late on Friday evenings, and they're really busy. I couldn't ask Mrs. Price to take me when not even her own daughter had pierced ears. I couldn't go by myself, because the store insisted you have someone with you if you were under eighteen, even with your parents' signature. I was wondering whether I should go to bed for three days or eat a whole box of chocolate-covered grahams, when Lester walked in.

I threw my arms around him. "Mo-ther!" I said.

"Huh?" said Lester.

"You've got to be mom-for-a-day, Les. Please! Mrs. Jones has the flu and can't take me to the jewelry store, and I have to be there at five-thirty. I've got Dad's permission slip and everything. All you have to do is drive me there and back."

I didn't think he'd do it. Lester doesn't like you to bug him when he first gets home from classes at the U. He opened a can of Sprite and chugged it down. Then he wiped one hand across his mouth.

"Straight there and back, no stops, no window shopping, zip, zip, chop, chop?" he asked.

I hugged him again. "I promise," I said.

We went out to the car.

"You know, don't you, Al," he said, backing down the drive, "that it's probably some primitive urge that has nothing to do with beauty."

"What?"

"Getting your ears pierced. Why don't you get your nose pierced while you're at it? Get seventeen brass rings to wear around your neck or something. If women only knew how ridiculous they look . . ."

"Marilyn and Crystal both had their ears pierced," I told him.

"That doesn't mean I approved."

"Lester, don't try to talk me out of it. My mind is made up."

He turned at the corner. "What if I told you studies show that piercing your ears is a form of self-mutilation that has more to do with self-loathing than self-love and is a last-ditch attempt to conform to a neurotic society?"

"I'd say it sounds like something you made up, Lester, and I'm going to do it, no matter what," I told him.

When we got downtown, Lester followed me into the jewelry store, and after I'd chosen my gold studs, he went to a room at the back with me, where a nurse motioned me up on a stool.

She showed me how to get the backs off the ear-rings, and explained how to take care of my ears for the first couple months. Then she held my face in her hands and carefully made little pen marks on each earlobe to make sure she had them even.

"Ready?" she asked, smiling.

I grinned and nodded. She put one of my gold studs in the stud gun. Then she rubbed an anesthetic on my earlobe. *Pop.* I felt a hard prick on one ear.

Thud. The nurse turned and we stared. Lester was flat on the floor, fainted dead away.

3

Losing Loretta

LESTER SAID later he had the flu, but he knew, and I knew, what made him faint. The nurse had asked him to sit down for ten minutes before she'd let him drive me home. I had the good sense not to tell either Pamela or Elizabeth about it, because I knew it would have embarrassed Lester. What I *didn't* have enough sense not to do was tell Loretta Jenkins.

At the time I didn't think it mattered. I headed for the Melody Inn the next morning to put in my three hours, as usual. I work for Dad on Saturdays doing whatever needs to be done: putting price stickers on sheet music, dusting the pianos, washing the glass on the revolving jewelry case in the Gift Shoppe, sweeping out the soundproof cubicles where kids come to take lessons. . . .

I couldn't wait to get to the store that morning, in fact. I zipped past Janice Sherman in sheet music with only a wave and didn't stop till I'd reached Loretta. Janice Sherman is like the mother superior of the Melody Inn, but Loretta's the big sister I never had. She isn't at all like Marilyn and Crystal, who are sort of elegant and classy. Loretta's got this curly hair like a sunburst around her head, and she chews gum. But her heart is so big and warm and open you could walk right in it. She has a great smile, a nice laugh, and she's good with customers, so even though she drives Dad nuts sometimes with her chatter, he keeps her on. I couldn't help liking her a lot.

"Look!" I said, and turned my head so she could see one of my gold studs.

"You *did* it!" she cried. "Oh, Alice, have I ever got the earrings for you!" She pressed the button that made the revolving wheel go around.

We both looked into the lighted case. Everything in the Melody Inn Gift Shoppe has to do with music, of course. There were little silver violin pins to wear on a suit; barrettes shaped like treble clefs; gold trumpet earrings; chain bracelets with dangly instruments; a gorgeous necklace of musical notes; and rings.

I liked the ceramic earrings that looked like banjos.

Loretta winked. "I'll put them away for you," she said, taking them out of the case so I could buy them when I'd saved enough. I grinned.

I was a half-grown woman now, with nonvirgin

earlobes, and I felt as though I'd been admitted to the Secret Society of Sisters or something. Whatever Loretta knew about life, she'd share with me, I was sure. I'd laugh like Loretta laughed, learn to talk free and easy with everyone who came in, just like she did.

It was as though the holes in my ears had opened a new world for me that could be summed up in one word: homogeneity. (I learned that in life science.) It means having identical functions or values. I wanted to be an identical twin to every girl in seventh grade. If we were all standing in a line that stretched around the entire state of Maryland, I didn't want anyone to be able to tell me from anyone else.

"Well, how did it go?" Loretta asked, as I took my rag and Windex and started cleaning the glass on the case. "Your ears are still a little red."

I grinned. "It hurt Lester more than it did me."

"Lester?"

I told her how he'd keeled over at the sound of the stud gun and had a lump on one side of his head. Loretta laughed.

"Well, he's got a lot of girlfriends to take care of him," she said, rearranging the row of coffee mugs on the shelf behind her, each with a picture of a composer on them.

"Wrong," I said. "Right now he hasn't got any."

"What's the matter? Les losing his touch?"

"He couldn't decide between Marilyn and Crystal, so he's going solo awhile."

"Umm," said Loretta, and I figured she'd probably been in the same situation herself with boyfriends.

"He still play the guitar?" she asked.

I nodded. "Especially now that he's not going out so much."

"Umm," she said again.

That evening, Dad, Lester, and I were cleaning out the refrigerator, which hadn't been done since we'd moved in a year and a half ago. Dad had kept setting a date for us to do it, and we kept putting it off, so finally he said that no one was leaving the house until we'd gone through our Westinghouse shelf by shelf.

Dad took things out one at a time, and of course Lester and I claimed we'd never seen them before in our lives. Taking the foil off a saucer you'd been missing for three months was like looking beneath a large rock out by the alley.

"Spinach," Lester guessed.

"No, it's not," I said. "It's lima beans with something growing on top."

"Out," said Dad, and tipped the saucer over the garbage pail.

"Hey, *there's* the rest of my birthday cake!" I cried when Dad pulled out a waxed carton from the back of the vegetable bin. "I *knew* I hid it somewhere!"

Dad studied the package in his hand. "It says 'corn.'"

"That's so Lester wouldn't find it."

"Al, your birthday was eight months ago!"

"So I forgot."

We had only done the lower shelf and half the vegetable bin when the doorbell rang.

I went to answer while Les and Dad argued over who had put an opened tin of sardines in the cheese compartment. As I crossed the living room, I glanced out the window overlooking the porch. Loretta Jenkins.

Suddenly everything clicked. The questions, the answers, the long, thoughtful "Umms." I temporarily forgot the Sisterhood.

"Lester, run for your life!" I cried.

"What?" Lester came to the doorway of the kitchen, holding an unmentionable something.

The doorbell rang again.

"Who is it?" called Dad.

"Loretta Jenkins!"

"So let her in," he said.

You'd think that after all the problems Dad and Les had been through in their love lives lately, they would have realized there was a new problem standing just outside the door. But Lester had to open it.

"Hi!" said Loretta, and her perfume hit me in the face.

"How you doin'?" Lester said. "Come on in."

Loretta stepped inside. "I don't know if you have this by Jimi Hendrix, but I thought you might like to try it, Les," she said, holding out some sheet music. And then, seeing Dad in the dining room, she called, "I paid for it myself, Mr. M."

Dad smiled and went back to the kitchen.

"Well . . . thanks!" Lester said, looking around for a place to set the bowl. Loretta simply took it from him and gave him the guitar music.

"Hey, this looks great!" said Lester, leafing through the pages. "I'll give it a try. Thanks a lot."

Loretta walked over and sat down. "I'm glad you like it. As soon as I saw the music, I thought of you." She studied the bowl in her lap. "What *is* this?"

"Don't open it!" I yelped, but it was too late. She'd lifted one corner of the tinfoil. "Oh, m'gosh!" she gasped. "Science project?"

What it was, I discovered, was the squash-and-onion casserole Dad had made last August and said he was going to serve every meal until it was gone.

"Sorry about that," I told her and whisked it away. And then, because I knew Les would need help, I went back to the living room.

". . . lobster and shrimp," Loretta was saying as I plopped down in the beanbag chair in one corner. "Mother said that when I was little I was allergic to everything but water and air."

I didn't know how the conversation got from Jimi Hendrix to lobster and shrimp, but you put a nickel in Loretta, you can't shut her up.

"Lester used to throw up if he ate anything with eggs in it," I said, trying to bring the conversation to a quick close. I felt responsible for Loretta's coming over. But that didn't work with Loretta.

"I used to throw up if I ate anything before eight

in the morning," she said. "Wake up, eat breakfast, throw up, go to school; wake up, eat breakfast, throw up . . ."

Lester's eyes glazed over.

All at once I cried, "Lester, look at the time!"

He stared at me.

"Almost six-thirty!" I insisted, looking at him hard.

And suddenly Lester snapped to.

"Ye gods," he said, leaping up. "I'm outta here! Thanks a lot, Loretta. Hendrix I'm not, but I'll fool around with that music."

"I hope I'm not keeping you from anything," Loretta said, fishing for information.

"If I hurry, I can still make it," Lester said in answer, and took out his car keys. "Be home late, Dad," he called.

Loretta followed him out to his car, even hanging over the door until he finally turned the key in the ignition. She waved him around the corner, then got in her own car and drove off.

It was fifteen minutes later, as Dad and I were throwing out something purple, that Lester walked in the back door.

"Thanks a bunch, Al," he said, taking off his jacket. "Was that just my imagination, or was she coming on to me?"

"It wasn't your imagination," I told him. "If you'd been sitting on the couch, she would have been in your lap."

Les turned to Dad. "Did I encourage her? Have I

ever said one thing to Loretta to make her think I was hitting on her?"

"Maybe she thinks you need a woman in your life," I suggested.

"I don't need any women," Lester said. "I haven't dated anyone since Christmas."

"That's three weeks. Should we call the *Guinness Book of World Records*?" Dad asked.

"I'm serious," said Les. "I'm going to prove that I can get through my junior year without any chicks messing me up. Just once, I'd like to be able to say I made the dean's list."

"Bravo!" said Dad. "That would please me, Lester; it really would."

Lester looked at me. "So if Loretta comes by again, Al, tell her I've gone to Mexico, will you? Tell her anything. Just lose her for me."

I began to wonder, though, if Lester would ever find the right girl. He always seemed to be out on weekends but never settled on anyone in particular. What if none was ever good enough because the girl he was really looking for was Mom? I read that in a magazine once. The article was "Can This Marriage Be Saved?"

When Dad finally left the kitchen and Les and I were mopping up, I said, "Les, what's the very first thing you think of when I say 'Marilyn'?" (If his answer was homemade cookies, I'd know we had a real case on our hands.)

"You don't want to know, Al," he said.

"Yes, I do."

"Well, I'm not going to tell you, snoop! It's none of your business."

"Okay, then, what's the first thing that comes to mind when I say 'Crystal'?"

Lester whistled through his teeth. "Wow! You *really* don't want to know that. Don't ask!"

So much for the test. Maybe losing a mom was different for boys than it was for girls.

Losing Loretta, though, was even harder than I'd thought. She called the next day and wanted to know if Lester had tried the music yet. Lester said he'd been sort of busy, but he'd let her know. She called the night after that, and as soon as I told Les it was Loretta, he holed up in the bathroom. I told her he was indisposed.

"What are we going to do, Dad?" Lester said after Loretta had called every night for a week. "Can't you fire her or something?"

"Now, you know I can't do that, Les. You're smart enough to handle this. Tell her you're going through a sort of introspective period right now—doing a lot of heavy thinking: a retreat for the soul or something."

"Surely you joke," said Lester.

It sounded pretty good to me, though, because Lester really was doing a lot of reading lately. He was taking a philosophy course at the university and reading books called *The Condition of Man* and *An Enquiry Concerning Human Understanding.* So on Saturday, when I put in my three hours again at the Melody Inn, and Loretta asked whether Lester had tried the music yet, I said, "It's not that he doesn't want to, he's just buried in his books right now. He's going through"—I tried to remember what Dad had called it—"a dark night of the soul." That didn't sound right, but I think I'd heard it somewhere.

"Really?" Loretta was dusting a little plaster bust of Beethoven. "In what way, Alice?"

"He's doing a lot of thinking and reading, and has a lot of decisions to make about his life. That's why he's not going out with women right now."

Loretta put Beethoven down and stared at me. "He's given up *women*?"

"Almost." I nodded.

"Alice, is he . . . well, studying for the priesthood or something?" She looked at me intently.

I'd not even thought of that but decided we couldn't actually rule it out. "It's a possibility," I told her.

"For heaven's sake!" Loretta said. "I'd never have thought it of Lester. I can't believe it!"

"Me, either," I said.

That night, Dad was spreading out his income tax stuff on the folding table in our dining room.

"Does our church have priests?" I asked from the doorway.

"No, Al. Now, you know that."

I didn't, really. "Would we have to join another church for Les to become a priest?"

"Of course! Lester would, anyway. But that's about the most unlikely thing I can think of."

"But it *could* happen?"

"Yes, and I could be on the first space shuttle to Mars," he said.

On Monday I was watching TV, Dad was filling out more income tax forms, and Lester was up in his room doing calculus. The doorbell rang and I looked out to see Loretta.

"Great God in heaven, not again!" said Dad when I told him, and he buried his head in his hands. "Tell Les he's got to come down here. I simply cannot afford to get involved in that girl's chatter."

I opened the door.

"I just came to see Les for a moment. I can't stay long," Loretta said.

I went upstairs. "Lester, Loretta's here and says she can't stay long."

"I've got a test tomorrow, Al! Tell her I'm vomiting. I'm unconscious! Unconsciously contagious! Tell her anything!"

"Dad says you've got to handle this. He's doing the income tax," I told him. And then I went in and stood by his bed. "Listen to me, Lester. All you have to do is put on a dark turtleneck shirt, carry a book with you, and don't smile. What*ever* you do, Lester, don't smile."

"You're talking nuts."

"Do you want to get rid of Loretta?" I asked.

"Is the pope Catholic?" Lester said in return, and I was glad he put it that way.

He got up, pulled off his orange sweatshirt with the Budweiser label on the front, and pulled on his black turtleneck.

"Why am I doing this?" he said.

"Don't ask." I handed him his copy of *The Critique of Pure Reason.* "And don't smile!" I whispered as he started downstairs.

Loretta was still in the hallway, cracking her gum, but as soon as she saw Lester, she stopped chewing.

"Lester," she said softly, "I didn't mean to disturb you, but I just wanted to say I understand."

Lester stood stone still.

"And I brought you something . . . well, I just thought this might help." She handed him a cassette, and from where I stood on the step behind him, I saw that it was the Mormon Tabernacle Choir singing *Climb Every Mountain.*

"Thank you," said Lester, looking puzzled.

"I paid for them myself, Mr. M.," Loretta called to Dad. Then, "Good night, Alice. 'Night, Les."

The door closed behind her, and Lester stared at the cassettes in his hands. "What in the world . . . ?" he asked, turning to me.

"For your dark night of the soul," I told him, and went back to watch TV.

4

Zombie Girls

I WAS sorry the next day that I'd let Loretta down, though. All she was guilty of was liking Lester, and I felt torn between my loyalty to womankind and to Dad and Les. If I was a true Sister, wouldn't I have paid more attention to *her* feelings? Tried to see things from Loretta's point of view? What was the good of Sisterhood if you always sided with a guy just because he happened to be your brother?

To make up for it, I made an announcement at breakfast: "I think you ought to know that I consider myself a member of the Sisterhood—all for one and one for all."

Lester groggily raised his head over his cup of coffee. "What is this, a declaration of war?"

"All I'm saying is that now I'm a half-grown woman—"

"Which half?" asked Lester.

I ignored him. "I want to do what other women do, feel what other women feel, experience everything there is to experience. . . ." I knew it was wild.

"That could be rather dangerous, couldn't it?" said Dad. "What did you have in mind?"

I shrugged. "Nothing yet."

"You won't do anything without talking to me first, will you?"

"Like what?" I asked.

Dad smiled a little. "Oh, dye your hair purple or something?"

"I'll talk to you first," I promised.

Somehow I'd had the idea that I'd have all new classes and teachers when the new semester began near the end of January. When I was talking to some of the other kids in homeroom, though, they told me that only the electives change. The major courses go right on as they were before—same room, same class, same teacher.

I was glad I'd still have Miss Summers, of course. *Every*one who had Miss Summers was glad. She taught eighth and ninth graders too, and I hoped I'd get lucky and have her all through junior high. When I realized I'd have Mr. Hensley some more, though, I groaned. I leaned over the aisle in homeroom and pretended to barf, and it must have been a realistic performance, because it got a big laugh from the other kids: a series of short gags followed by Mount Vesuvius.

Actually, I felt a little sorry for Mr. Hensley and tried my best to pay attention in class. Once in a while, though, when he gave an incredibly dull assignment, I'd pretend to vomit, and it always got a big laugh. Hensley would look around from the blackboard, confused, never knowing what brought it on.

The nice thing that happened, though, was that one of the other world studies classes had too many kids in it; three of them were transferred over to Hensley for the second semester, and one of them was Pamela. Last semester I hadn't had any classes with her at all. She was especially glad because Mark Stedmeister was in my class—Mark and three other guys who were all good-looking but goofy. (I called them the Three Handsome Stooges; Pamela called them the best-looking guys in seventh grade.)

I was still in the same gym class with Elizabeth, of course. As for electives, when I went from nutrition to gourmet cooking (you have to take nutrition before you get cooking), I found Pamela, Patrick, and two of the Stooges in my class. So things were definitely a little more interesting this semester. Not to mention the fact that *I* was more interesting—my earlobes, anyway.

I loved waking up in the mornings to find that the little gold studs were still there. Every day I wiggled them around in my earlobes, squeezed a ball of cotton soaked in hydrogen peroxide between each earring and its hole, and made sure that the backs were still on correctly. Then I put on my Levi's, my Gap shirt, my Britches of Georgetowne sweater, my Esprit socks, and my Nikes, and went out to wait for the bus like all the other seventh-grade girls in the country. Well, *almost* like all the other girls. According to Pamela, I wasn't there yet.

"You don't *belong* to anything, Alice!" she said. "How can you be a part of the seventh-grade experience when you haven't even joined any clubs?"

"Maybe next year," I said. "It's too late now, isn't it?"

"You can always join the All-Stars Fan Club," said Pamela.

"What do I have to do?"

"Just come to room twenty-one B every Wednesday after school. We write fan letters and trade ideas on how to get photos and autographs from famous people."

"Who?"

"Movie stars, football players, rock stars. . . . Sometimes we write to authors, because they most always answer, but this week a bunch of us are writing to the Velvet Pistols. You should see Izzy, their drummer! He's one to die for!"

I tried to imagine throwing myself off a cliff for somebody named Izzy. Still, if I could get an autographed poster or something, it would fill up half my bulletin board. . . .

At five after three that Wednesday, I was sitting on one of the desks in 21B when the other kids trooped in. One of the typing teachers sponsors the club, and when she's not there, Pamela told me, Brian Brewster (one of the Handsome Stooges) takes over.

Someone waved an autograph she got from Tom Cruise, but Pamela showed me a newspaper photo of the Velvet Pistols. *"This,"* she said, "is Izzy."

I stared at the picture of five men in tight leather shorts and cowboy hats, their chests bare. They all had long, curly hair, with rings in their ears and on the sides of their noses, and I wondered if I could stand to look at Izzy the Drummer every morning and evening for the rest of junior high school if he *did* send a poster. He had a tattoo of a pistol on one arm, a skeleton on the other.

"Aren't they wonderful?" sighed Pamela.

After the sacred relics were passed around, we started our fan letters.

"Make it *different*," said Brian Brewster. "If it stands out from all the rest, somebody will notice."

I decided to write the wildest one I could, but not mail it.

Pamela finished first and read her letter aloud for comment:

Dear Izzy:

Do you know how many times I have dreamed about you in the past month? Nineteen. I want you, want you, want you; need you, need you, need you. I adore you, darling Izzy, and can never be happy unless I have your picture to look at always. If you would autograph it too, or just send an autographed poster, I'd be delirious.

Pamela Jones

If Pamela wanted, needed, and adored Izzy, I wondered, how could she be happy with only a poster?

"It's okay, Pam, but 'I adore you' is sort of old. Write something with a little more pizzazz," Brian told her.

I was just writing mine for a joke, so I didn't care.

"Dear Breath of Life," I scribbled. "I am looking at a picture of you from the paper. I worship the hair on your legs, the veins on your temples, the pistol tattoo on your biceps." I tapped the pencil on the desk and grinned as I wrote the next line: "I love your sweat; your saliva; the dirt beneath your fingernails—even worship your dandruff, if you have any—the lint in your belly button." I smiled to myself. "Please, my precious, send a poster for my very own, so that I may experience ecstasy everlasting. Your passionate playmate, Alice McKinley."

Pamela reached over and snatched the letter from my hand. "What are you laughing at?" she asked, and then, to the others, "Alice is through with hers."

"No!" I said, but she held me off.

"Listen up," she called, and read it aloud.

"Oh, my *gosh!*" said one of the girls. "Did you really mean what you said about the lint in his belly button? Alice, what if he doesn't *have* any lint in his belly button?"

"It's wonderful!" proclaimed Brian. "No revision necessary!" And he passed it along to the girl at the envelope table, who addressed it, stamped it, and dropped it into our letter box. I was glad Elizabeth wasn't a member of the All-Stars Fan Club. If she had heard my letter she would have passed out on the floor.

"Lester," I said at dinner that evening, "what's the chance of getting an answer if you write a rock star?"

"About the same as getting hit on the head by a meteorite," he said.

I didn't know if I was glad or sorry. I'd be embarrassed if I thought Izzy actually read my letter, but it would be sort of nice to have a poster of him on my bulletin board and see Pamela's face when she walked into my room. *I* might not be able to stand him, but a lot of other girls could, and they'd all come by to see him, especially if it was Izzy in his shorts.

"You're writing to rock stars, Al?" asked Dad, as he served the jambalaya. I think there's a real recipe for this somewhere, but in our house it's made with whatever leftover meat and vegetables we find in the refrigerator, mixed in the skillet with a raw egg. If it looks pretty good when it's done, Dad serves it over rice. If it doesn't, he hides it in a bun. Tonight's jambalaya was served in a huge hard roll, so I didn't bother to peek.

"Oh, Pamela's been trying to get a poster of the Velvet Pistols, so I wrote a letter too," I said.

Lester was about to take a bite of salad, but he lowered his fork. "The *Velvet Pistols!* Ye gods, Al!"

Dad turned around. "What do you see in *them*, Al? Of all the rock groups you could have picked . . ."

"I don't even *know* them!" I said, plunking down my glass. "Pamela just wants a picture of the drummer, so I joined this fan club. . . ."

"You don't even know the group, and you write for a picture of the drummer?" asked Dad.

Now I was getting defensive. "So what do *you* know about them?"

"A sales rep was by with some promotional material, and I took a look at some of their lyrics. Mercifully, I can't remember anything more than a feeling of profound disgust," said Dad.

" 'Zombie Girls,' for starters," offered Lester, and proceeded to recite it for me:

"Turn 'em over once,
Turn 'em over twice,
Havin' sex with zombie girls
Is really kinda nice."

I stared. "*Dead* people?" I asked.

"No, that's another song—'My Necrophiliac Lover,' " said Lester. "This one's about making out with girls who are drunk or stoned."

"See what I mean?" said Dad.

I blushed, and I'm not even Elizabeth. "If they're so

awful, why do you even have their music in your store?"

"I don't. I didn't order any."

"That's censorship," I said. I don't know why I didn't just become a groupie for the Velvet Pistols, the way I was standing up for them.

"That's *selection*, Al. One store can't stock everything. I have to pick and choose, and I chose not to stock the Pistols. I didn't say nobody else could, either."

"It's not just their music," added Lester. "One of the band members was arrested for molesting a teenage girl, and they've also been fined for trashing a hotel room. Not exactly the sort you'd like to pin up on your wall. . . ."

"Okay, send me to a convent!" I squealed. "All I wanted was one lousy poster. You already told me I had as much chance of hearing from them as a meteorite falling on my head."

"Right. Falling on your head at exactly one minute past seven on Saint Patrick's Day, to be exact," said Les, and grinned.

I didn't tell them what I'd actually *said* in the letter. If I did that I'd probably be sent to the Sacred Heart of Our Blessed Mary Middle School by morning. If Aunt *Sally* knew what I'd written, I'd be in a convent before the evening was out.

What I was most concerned about at the moment was taking off my earrings for the first time and getting them back on again. After two weeks, you're supposed to take them off once a day.

The coming-out ceremony took place that Friday in the girls' rest room over lunch period. Pamela said that the first thing to do was close the stopper in the sink so that your earrings couldn't fall down the drain. I didn't have any trouble taking the backs off and pulling the studs out, even though my earlobes were still sensitive, but putting the studs back in again was a different matter. No matter how I turned my head, I couldn't find the holes.

"You just sort of have to poke around with one finger behind your ear so you'll know when the end is coming through," instructed Pamela.

I could see Elizabeth in the mirror, backed up against the wall.

"I have better luck when I wet the earlobe with my finger," said a girl named Jill. "It makes the hole stand out." But I still couldn't do it. My earlobe was feeling worse by the minute, as none of the jabs went through. One of the holes began to ooze a little blood. Elizabeth was turning pale.

"You've got to get them back in before the bell," said a girl who was washing her hands farther down. "If you don't put them in when your ears are oozing like that, the holes will close up for sure."

"This is so gross!" said Elizabeth. "I am never going to pierce my ears as long as I live. I don't care if boys never ask me out. I don't care if I'm the only one who doesn't go to the prom. They'd have to knock me out and—"

"Shut up, Elizabeth," said Pamela. "We've almost got one in." She put the left earring in, but not the one on the right. The bell rang.

"What you have to figure out," said Jill, coming over, "is which way the hole slants. Each hole is different. Once you figure out how they slant, you can guide the stud in a little better."

My ears were burning now, and I could feel angry tears in my eyes. How could I have thought it would be as simple as hanging Christmas ornaments on a tree? Pamela managed to get the second stud in place, and I finally made it to language arts, my earlobes fiery red. Even Miss Summers noticed.

"New earrings?" she asked.

I nodded.

"Nice," she said.

After that I felt terrific just thinking about the way the girls had fussed over me there in the rest room, the way they'd helped and encouraged me. I'd been surrounded with Sisters, I realized, and now the most beautiful Sister of all had said, "Nice." I beamed.

The following Wednesday, when I entered 21B, I was surrounded again.

"You got a reply!" one of the All-Stars Fan Club girls shrieked. "It's from New York."

I couldn't imagine how someone else would know that I got a letter. Then I remembered that our fan mail was sent out with the school address in the upper left corner so that all the replies came here.

While Pamela and the other members gathered around me, I examined the envelope. It was bulky—

obviously something more than a letter, but impossibly small for a poster.

"Open it!" Pamela screeched.

I did, and it smelled awful. Inside was a dirty sock, with a note pinned to the top: "Sweat and all. You got it, kid. Izzy."

5

Sex

I WAS suddenly "in." No one in the club had ever received a personal item from a rock star before, and they crowded around me as though I had just won the lottery. What I knew positively, however, was that I did not want to pin Izzy's sock on my bulletin board, Sisterhood or not.

"I could always wash it, I suppose," I said.

You'd think I had suggested whitewashing the Mona Lisa. "No!" chanted the girls beside me. "Alice, don't! Not ever! You told him you loved his sweat, and he sent you some."

"If I'd wanted a smelly sock, I could have borrowed my brother's," I told them.

"Sell it!" said Brian. "Auction it off."

Which is why, the following day, there was a notice on the school bulletin board, saying:

TO BARTER, TRADE, OR SELL
One used sock belonging to
Izzy Herrigan of the Velvet Pistols.
Autograph included.
Best offer.
Alice McKinley, room 46A.

So this is what it's like to be popular, I thought, as people stopped me in the halls all day to make offers. The highest offer was fifty dollars and the lowest was a gerbil. I finally traded it to Pamela for two pairs of fourteen-karat gold earrings, and she said she was keeping the sock under the plastic dome of a cheese server, sort of a shrine, I guess. Seventh grade sure is weird.

Take the unit we were studying in health, for example: Our Changing Bodies. Boys took it too, only in separate classes. We took the class from Mrs. Bolino, who's gorgeous. Not exactly the kind you'd go to with a problem, but gorgeous. The boys took it from Mr. Parks, the basketball coach, who looks like Paul Newman with black hair. If Mrs. Bolino wasn't already married, we figure she'd be dating Mr. Parks. What the unit was all about, of course, was sex, but you can't exactly label a course sex 101, so twice a week we sat in a room next to the gym to learn about Our Changing Bodies.

You had to have a note from home before you could take the course, and Elizabeth didn't really want to, but her mother made her, which is surprising. Her mother said that if she didn't learn it in school she might pick it up on the street. I've heard that before but I've never understood. I look out our window and don't see a single person who would start talking to me about sex just because I didn't study it in school. Anyway, Elizabeth and I sat beside each other, and as soon as Mrs. Bolino began, Elizabeth wrapped her arms tightly around her body, as though she wasn't about to let *hers* do any changing, ready or not.

For the past week we'd been studying the female reproductive system, and when we got to class on Friday, there was a surprise quiz. The teacher gave each of us a diagram of a woman's reproductive organs, and we had to label everything in sight. We set to work, trying to decide if the little flowery thing at the end of the fallopian tube had a name, when the door opened and Mr. Parks walked in, looking for the volleyball net.

And suddenly, like a pack of starlings, girls started screeching and covering their diagrams. I think Elizabeth started it, actually, but the scream went around the room like a brush fire. A couple girls even leaned over and bodily protected their ovaries and fallopian tubes from the astonished gaze of Mr. Parks.

The coach got the volleyball net in a hurry, and after he left the room, Mrs. Bolino faced us, frowning.

"Girls," she said. "I hope . . . most sincerely . . . that I will never again witness what has just gone on in this room. You negate yourselves when you put on a display like that. To cover the drawings of your own reproductive organs shows that you feel there is something embarrassing about your sex. If you are embarrassed about your sex, it must mean that you feel there is something demeaning or disgusting about being female. You are all wondrously made, girls. Remember that: wondrously made, and you should carry your sex proudly, a badge of honor."

I simply could not help myself. I tucked one edge of the paper under my chin so that the diagram of the reproductive organs covered my chest, and then I stood up and raised my arms above my head like a champion: I was proudly carrying my sex.

I shouldn't have tried that with Mrs. Bolino.

"A wonderful idea, Miss McKinley," she said. "Since you were so taken with my lecture, you may tape the diagram to your chest and wear it to your next class."

There was absolute quiet in the room. I stared. The girls gaped. If Mrs. Bolino really, truly believed that there was nothing embarrassing about our sexual organs, why was she making me wear them as punishment?

She got some tape from her drawer, and after checking my answers, taped the diagram to my T-shirt. When the bell rang, I walked out into the hall.

There was nothing to stop me from tearing it off, of course, and I suspect Mrs. Bolino figured I would.

"Take it *off,* Alice!" Elizabeth begged, when we'd turned the corner. "She's *awful!* You don't have to wear that! You know you don't."

But I'm stubborn too, sometimes. If she told me to

wear the darn diagram, I'd do it. Elizabeth wouldn't walk beside me, though. I guess she figured that if anybody hadn't known we had fallopian tubes, she didn't want them to know now, so she walked as far ahead of me as she could get.

I was going to get even with Mrs. Bolino by wearing the paper all day, and hoped the principal would stop me in the hall so I could tell him about this cruel and unusual punishment. But by the time the day was half over, the momentum had worn off and the paper was torn and wrinkled. Kids who knew nothing about the Our Changing Bodies quiz thought I was weird. But I wanted Patrick to see it before I took it off, so I wore it to gourmet cooking. Patrick has traveled all around the world with his folks; they're diplomats or something. He probably thinks that nothing exciting ever happens to me, so I marched in with my reproductive organs on my chest.

"What's that all about?" he asked, when I sat down at our workstation. We're partners when we use the stove. "I saw you wearing it in the hall this morning."

"Mrs. Bolino made me do it for smarting off," I said.

He studied the diagram, turning his head sideways. "The cervix. You missed that one."

I felt my face redden. "How do you know?" I demanded. He didn't even have a sister!

"Because we finished the unit on male organs last week and have already started the female."

That meant that *we* were going to study male organs next. I pulled the diagram off my chest and threw it into the trash. I decided I wanted to sit right behind Elizabeth in that class so that when she fell over backward I could catch her.

Meanwhile, however, I felt like a drip. Especially when one of the Three Handsome Stooges found my paper in the wastebasket. He started smirking and whispering with the other boys, and I wished for all the world I'd crumpled that diagram up and stuck it in my book bag.

What was worse, we were cooking liver that day, and we figured we'd been tricked. The first day of gourmet cooking we'd made pizza, and that was okay. But now we realized that gourmet cooking was just another name for nutrition. The difference was that last semester we'd divided food into the four basic food groups, and this semester we had to cook it. On this day each workstation was given a glistening slab of dark red liver, which sat quivering on our countertop like an organ waiting to be transplanted.

The instructor had gone to the door to take a message, when the Stooge who had found my diagram picked up his piece of liver, dangled it by one end, and said to a boy across the room, "Hey, Jim! Placenta! Catch!" And gave it a toss. From there it went to Patrick, then to a guy over by the window, and by the time the teacher stopped the show, the liver had been under the radiator, in the wastebasket, and had left a wet spot on the blackboard.

Some of the girls were glaring at me for bringing our reproductive organs to class. I swiveled around on my stool and faced the liver.

"I don't think I can stand this, Patrick," I said as he floured and seasoned it the way the teacher told us, then pounded it with the edge of a saucer to make it tender.

"It's okay. I'll eat yours," he said. Patrick, who has traveled everywhere and eaten squid in Japan, came to the rescue once again.

I ate the two obligatory bites you have to take to pass, however, and it wasn't half bad.

The beginning of February, in Washington, D.C.—which is only a few miles from Silver Spring—is about the ugliest time of year. Nothing's in bloom, of course, and all you can see are monuments and buildings, which is why Aunt Sally decided to come. There wouldn't be any tourists around, she said, and she could have the city to herself. The main reason was that Carol was flying to Washington to attend a three-day conference, and Aunt Sally decided to come along and see for herself how well or how poorly we were running our lives without Mom.

It was a whirlwind trip. Each morning, Dad would drive Aunt Sally and Carol to the Metro. Aunt Sally went to the museums and Carol went to her conference. Each night, Les would pick them up, and then we'd go out to dinner or a movie or something. I figured I could live like this a long time.

We were at a Mexican restaurant the second night, though, when I embarrassed Lester by asking the waiter whether the dish I'd ordered had any "jallopeeno" peppers in it.

"That's pronounced hal-a-*pain*-yo," Lester told me after the waiter was gone.

"Then why does it start with a *j*?" I asked.

"Because it's Spanish, Al," said Dad. "Aren't you taking any foreign languages?"

"Not till high school," I told him.

"What you've got to remember is that a *j* in Spanish sounds like an *h,* just like a *w* in German sounds like a *v*," Lester told me. "And a *v* in German sounds like an *f.*"

I thought about that awhile. "Then why isn't Volkswagen pronounced 'Folks-vagen'?" I said. Nobody seemed to know. Ha! I stumped them on that.

Aunt Sally cleared her throat. "Ben, it's hard for me to believe you didn't even know Alice wasn't taking a foreign language. Don't you help her choose her courses?"

"Not unless she asks," Dad said. "She has counselors at school, and they tell her what's required. If she has any questions, she can always come to me. Right, Al?"

"Right," I said.

Aunt Sally sat back as the waiter put some tortilla chips and salsa on the table, then leaned forward again. "What *are* you taking in seventh grade, Alice? Your mother certainly would have been interested in knowing."

"Our Changing Bodies," I told her. "We're just finishing fallopian tubes and we're getting ready for testicles."

I don't know if Aunt Sally ate her soup or not. I spent the rest of dinner talking to Carol.

The really nice part of their visit was that Carol slept in my bed and I slept on an old army cot beside her. Dad gave Aunt Sally his bed and he took the sofa. Les didn't have to give up his room because that would have meant cleaning it first, and we hadn't had a two-week notice.

Once the light was out, Carol didn't mind talking for a while in the dark, and I liked that. It's a lot easier to talk in the dark. The words sort of slide out and you're not entirely responsible.

The last night Carol was there, I asked, "Was my mom at all like yours?"

I heard the springs squeak and knew that Carol was turning over on her side, facing me. "She was a lot younger than my mother, not quite so set in her ways. I didn't know her all that well, Alice, but what I knew of Aunt Marie, I liked."

"Such as what?"

"Her sense of humor, for one thing. She was funny. Mother always takes things too seriously. I remember once"—Carol giggled a little—"I think we had just moved, and your mom came over to help us unpack. You must have been about one year old, so you stayed home with your dad. But Aunt Marie had climbed up on a step stool, leaned too far, and the whole thing went over. She broke her leg. I remember how Mom wouldn't let her move or anything—called an ambulance—and

I can still see your mother lying on the floor, wincing. It was summer—a really hot summer—and she had on a light skirt. Well, when the ambulance arrived, the paramedics had to examine her briefly before they moved her. I remember that one of the men said, 'Ma'am, excuse me, but I'm going to have to raise your skirt.' And despite the pain, your mom looked up at him with that mischievous spark in her eye and said, 'Will you still respect me in the morning?' "

Both Carol and I burst out laughing. I lay there smiling up at the ceiling, trying to imagine the whole thing—my mom saying something like that.

"But you know what?" Carol went on. "Mother never got the joke. She said she didn't see what there was to laugh about when someone was being rushed off to the emergency room. Anyway, that was one of the differences between your mom and mine."

Mom, I said silently in the dark, I would have liked you a lot. I mean, I do like you a lot. Everything I've found out about you. I thought of how Mother would have laughed about me going around school wearing my fallopian tubes on my chest.

"Poor Mum," Carol was saying. "Sometimes I think she would have been happier living in another century. She and Queen Victoria would have gotten along fine."

The next day, on the way to the airport, Aunt Sally said, "This has been a wonderful visit, Ben. Thanks for everything. Now tell me: Are you really, truly happy?"

Dad smiled. I could see his face in the rearview

mirror. "Well, Lester and Alice will have to speak for themselves, but happiness is relative, you know. From day to day, I'm in and out of happiness, but most of the time I'm content, if that's any comfort to you, Sal."

"I miss Marie, Ben."

"So do I, Sal."

While Dad was playing the piano that evening, and Lester and I were scrounging the kitchen for potato chips, I said, "I really like Carol. She's easy to talk to."

"Yeah, she's cool," Lester said.

"How old is she, do you figure?"

"Oh, probably twenty-three. She's been out of college for a couple years now."

"Do you think she's ever had sexual intercourse?"

Lester stared at me. "She was married awhile, Al. Didn't you know that?"

"Oh." I'd forgotten.

"Some guy in the navy. It only lasted a year," Lester said.

I sat in the kitchen after Lester left, thinking about that. I had actually been in a room all by myself with a woman who had experienced sexual intercourse, and I'd missed my chance to ask her what it was like. I'll bet she would have told me too. Especially in the dark.

I don't think I needed information nearly as much as Elizabeth needed it, though. She called me about nine that night.

"Alice," she whispered into the phone. "I've got to come over. I want to tell you something."

I met her at the door. She wouldn't even come up to my room. She said she couldn't talk inside the house at all, so we went down to the corner and leaned against the mailbox.

"What *is* it?" I asked.

"I can't believe this," said Elizabeth. "I never expected it to happen."

"*What?*"

"A baby," she said.

I gaped, my mouth opened. "*You're* . . . having . . . a *baby?*"

"No!" Elizabeth glared at me. "Of *course* not! My mother is, and I just can't believe . . . can't imagine . . . well, you know . . . that they did *that!*"

I was still staring. "Then how did you think *you* got here, Elizabeth? Federal Express?"

"But that was a long time ago, right after they were married. I didn't think they still . . ." She swallowed.

Sometimes I feel very grown up compared to Elizabeth. Sometimes I feel toward Elizabeth what Carol must feel toward me. Like a sister. I put my arm around her and walked her back to her house.

"What am I going to *tell* everyone?" she gulped.

"Believe me, you don't have to explain anything. Sooner or later folks will just know, that's all," I said.

"But . . . I thought . . . I thought you did it when you wanted children, and when you were . . . you know . . . through having children, you stopped."

"Elizabeth," I said, "if you ever need a vacation—I mean, if you ever want to get away from all this—you could go to Chicago and stay with Aunt Sally. She'd love to have you. You two would get along great. You really would."

6

Friends

I DECIDED that Sisterhood was one of the easiest things in the world. All I had to do was look out for other girls, and they'd look out for me.

Miss Summers was a member; Denise Whitlock, the large girl who sat in front of me in language arts, was a member; Loretta Jenkins; Janice Sherman; Aunt *Sally,* even! You were a member of the Universal Sisterhood whether you knew it or not. Like a big sorority, we were all in it together—old and young, fat and thin, pretty and plain—all you had to be was female and you were in. Being the only female member of my family, it was a great feeling to know I belonged to a group that understood what it's like to be a girl.

Of course, it was nicer to be a pretty Sister than a

plain one, and I never knew how much difference earrings could make until I looked in the mirror. One of the pairs Pamela had traded me had little green stones. I decided to wear them with a light green shirt Carol had given me, so the day after she left, I put them on. I'm not sure whether the earrings or the shirt highlighted the green in my eyes, but I thought, Not bad! Not bad at all!

Dad had left early for work, but Lester was still at the table.

"Les," I said, "how do I look?" I sat down across from him and leaned forward so he'd notice.

"Where?" he asked, looking at me hard. "You have a pimple or something?"

"No! I'm beautiful this morning, and you might have noticed."

"I noticed that your shirt is about three sizes too big."

"It's the fashion, Lester. Carol gave it to me."

"On Carol, anything looks great," he said.

The one person at school who noticed—other than Elizabeth and Pamela—was Miss Summers. I liked to think she gave me extra attention because she went to the Christmas concert with Dad and me last year, but I probably imagined it. When I walked in her room fourth period, she said, "Why, Alice, you're a symphony in green! You look lovely."

"Thanks," I told her, smiling. I never felt so elegant before.

Miss Summers, though, is a symphony in whatever

she wears. She can make ordinary gray look special. Blue is her best color, though, because of her eyes, so she wears that a lot. On this day she had on a blue lacy sweater over a blue skirt, with a white scarf thrown over one shoulder.

She was talking about how a biographer doesn't just list facts about his subjects but chooses events in that person's life which best reveal the type of person he or she is. Too often, in our own writing, she said, we clutter up the pages with things that aren't important. Then she gave us an assignment. To help us get to the heart of a personality, she wanted us to list all the members of our family, and then, beside each one, the title of a song or musical or book that best described that person. But we couldn't mix categories. We had to choose one and stick with it, for all the members of our family.

We smiled as we closed our books, and so did Miss Summers.

"This is a fun assignment, class," she said when the bell rang. "Enjoy."

Lester and I were the only ones at supper. He'd been lifting weights again in the basement and came to the table barefoot, in sweatpants. I hate it when he does that, because it makes the spaghetti taste like armpits.

"Where's Dad?" I asked, as I opened another can of tomato puree.

"I don't know," Lester said. "Working overtime, I guess. He called and said he'd be home around nine."

I told Lester about the English assignment. "I'm going to use the titles of musicals," I said. "I've got the perfect one for Dad: *The Music Man.*"

"Yeah?" Lester leaned over the pot and tasted the spaghetti sauce, then added some Tabasco. "What are you going to put beside your own name? Surely not *My Fair Lady?*"

"I can do without any help from you," I told him.

We were wolfing down the spaghetti and garlic bread (no salad; we never eat salad unless Dad is here to make it) when the doorbell rang. I thought maybe it was Dad with his arms full of groceries or something, and ran to open it.

There stood Lester's old girlfriend, Marilyn—his first true love—small, brown-haired, looking very pretty in tight knit pants and a furry jacket.

"Marilyn!" I said, delighted to see her. "Come on in. Lester and I were just finishing supper."

She smiled at me. "Wow, Alice! You look great. Pierced ears, and"—she made wavy motions with her hands—"you're getting a figure and everything." We both giggled.

I thought she'd sit down in the living room while I went to get Lester, but instead, she followed me through the dining room. Lester must not have heard us because he was stuffing a forkful of spaghetti in his mouth. When he saw Marilyn in the doorway, he swallowed it in one gulp.

"M-Marilyn!" he said, and wiped his mouth on the back of his hand. "For gosh sake!"

"Go right on with your dinner, Les, I've already eaten," Marilyn said, and her voice sounded like little bells. She pulled out a chair at the end of the table and sat down. "I was just driving by and thought, Why don't I stop? so I stopped."

"How you doin'?" Lester asked, and took another bite.

I think that's the difference between men and women. If *I* was sitting at the kitchen table barefoot, in sweatpants, with spaghetti sauce in the corners of my mouth, and Patrick walked in, I'd be up the stairs already. Lester, however, kept right on chewing.

"I'm doing all right," Marilyn said.

"Applesauce?" I asked, offering her the jar and spoon.

"No, thanks." She turned her attention to Les again. "How are *you* doing?"

"Studying hard. You know."

Marilyn nodded. Les nodded.

"They fixed up that old coffee shop down on Georgia Avenue—the one that used to have all those ferns in the window," Marilyn said. "Now they show silent movies in the evenings. It's fun. I thought you might like to walk over there, just for old time's sake. Have a cup of coffee."

"Uh . . . well . . ." Les looked about uncertainly.

"I'll do the dishes," I offered. I didn't know if I was helping or not, but I wanted Marilyn back at that moment almost more than anything else. I wanted a sister-in-law, so we could talk earrings and sex and love and life. But I didn't want Lester hurt again, and I didn't want Marilyn hurt, either.

"Let me put on some shoes," Lester said, and went upstairs.

I looked right at Marilyn. "How come you came back?" I asked. I had to know.

"Because I missed him."

Love, I am absolutely convinced, is the weirdest thing there is. Romantic love, I mean. "*What* did you miss?" I asked her. "Really."

"Oh, the way he sort of held me whenever I was worried about something. Real protective, you know. The whipped cream he puts in his coffee—sprays in his coffee, actually. I never see a can of Reddi Wip without thinking of Les. The way we could talk about all kinds of things. Just *him,* you know?" She glanced over at me. "Is he dating anyone else?"

"Not that I know of."

"Crystal Harkins?"

"No."

"I've got a chance then."

"As much as anyone else," I told her, and I noticed that when they walked out the front door together, she was clutching his arm. I mean, Lester probably hadn't even washed his armpits, and Marilyn was clutching his arm.

What would it be like to have another female in the house? I wondered. I mean, if Lester and Marilyn married and moved in upstairs or something? If mine weren't the only underpants and bras hanging on the line in the basement? If I wasn't the only one in the house with a menstrual cycle? If Dad could learn to treat hot curlers and panty liners like hot curlers and panty liners instead of small strange animals that lived in the cabinet under the sink?

I brought my notebook out to the kitchen table and wrote down the names of everyone in our family. I wrote *The Music Man* by Dad's name, *Li'l Abner* by Lester's, and I thought about my mom. Maybe I should call her *My Fair Lady,* but it didn't exactly fit. Then I remembered what Carol had told me about Mom joking with the paramedics. I smiled, and beside her name I wrote *Funny Girl.* The hardest title to come up with was the one for myself.

What Miss Summers wanted us to do was zero in on a major characteristic, like I'd done with the others. Music for Dad, bare feet for Lester, jokes for Mom. But me?

What's the first thing I think about when I think of myself? I wondered. I mean, if somebody else said I could tell them only one important thing about myself, what would it be? I knew before I even got to the end of the question. I was missing a mom.

"Alice McKinley," I wrote on my paper, and beside it I scribbled *Annie* (as in Little Orphan).

I cleaned up the kitchen, ate the rest of the spaghetti cold, and debated whether I should take a long, hot soak in the tub or make some banana pudding. The recipe was on the side of the vanilla wafer box, but by the time I read it to the end, I'd eaten half the wafers. So I went back to the living room to finish the chapter on hormones for the Our Changing Bodies unit.

It's amazing how grown up I began to feel, just knowing what all these hormones were getting ready to do inside me. I wondered when the names changed on the doors of rest rooms, from BOYS to MEN, and GIRLS to WOMEN. High school? College? Reaching puberty, I guess, is the next best thing to having a mother or sister. Your body marches in step with the other girls in your class, the hormones leading the way. I needed that—marching in step, I mean. I liked the feeling that I belonged.

The front door opened about eight-thirty, and I figured it was Dad coming in for dinner. It was Lester. "Guess what?" he said.

"You're engaged."

"Don't be dumb. We're friends again, nothing romantic. Just plain friends. Marilyn said it's ridiculous for us to go on not speaking."

"You were doing a good job of being friends before, until Marilyn discovered you were friends with Crystal Harkins too," I reminded him.

"Well, I think everything's clear now. You can be friends with a lot of people at the same time, and I'm sure Marilyn understands that," Les said. He took off his jacket and stretched out in a chair, smiling contentedly.

I propped my feet on the coffee table and studied my brother from across the room. "Les," I said, "Ann

Landers says that once people have sexual intercourse, it's almost impossible to make them stop."

Lester raised one eyebrow. "Who's talking sex here? Did I mention sex? I just said we were friends again, Al. That's all I said!"

"You sure?"

"Yes! And will you please stop saying 'sexual intercourse'? Just call it sex, for crying out loud."

"Okay, sex, then. You and Marilyn are now friends without sex?"

"She's got tickets for a folk concert, and we may go skiing—stuff like that," Lester told me.

I sighed. "Lester, listen to me. Marilyn is not interested in being just 'friends' with you. Marilyn is wearing a huge sign around her neck that says GO FOR IT." I wondered if I was being fair to the Sisterhood, but the fact was, I didn't want to see Marilyn hurt.

Les stared. "Go for what?"

"You, Lester. You!"

"I thought you liked Marilyn."

"I do! I *love* Marilyn! But a twenty-year-old woman is interested in more than folk concerts, especially a woman who has experienced sex," I told him. I never knew I was so profound. Ann Landers would have been proud of me.

"She tell you that, Al?"

"Hinted at it. You're going to get closer and closer to Marilyn until you are even *better* friends than before, and then you've got to decide all over again if it's going to be Marilyn for the rest of your life or if you're ever going out with girls like Crystal Harkins again."

There was a low, agonized moan from Lester. He stretched out in the chair until he was almost lying down and pulled his jacket up over his face. I decided I had enlightened him enough for one evening and went back to my chapter on hormones.

I wondered if Ann Landers was right. The way she made it sound, once you were into sex, it was like someone had put you in drive and there was no way to go into park or reverse or neutral until you reached your nineties or something.

When I looked up again, Lester's chair was empty, and I could hear him rummaging about in the kitchen. Then I heard a car out front, footsteps on the porch; Dad came inside.

"I was beginning to wonder!" I said, glancing at the clock. And when he didn't say anything, just hung up his coat, I said, "There *was* some spaghetti left, but I ate it."

He smiled. "That's okay. I already had dinner. How did things go today?"

"Fine," I told him. "For now, anyway. Marilyn came by to see Les tonight, so anything could happen in that department. But I had a great day." I waited for him to notice my green shirt and earrings, and when he didn't say anything, I got up and went to stand in the light where he could see me better.

"Look!" I said, and pointed to one of the green earrings I got from Pamela.

"Hey! Pretty sharp!" Dad said. "I really like them,

Al!" He looked me over. "You're a . . . a symphony in green!"

I stared at Dad. For ten seconds or so, my mind whirred like a computer. Then I blinked, my lips moved, and I heard my voice saying, "You're *dating*, Dad!" And before I could stop myself or even understand why, I ran upstairs and shut my door.

Things were changing, all right, and it wasn't just our bodies.

7

The Earring Club

I DIDN'T know if I was angry or surprised. Shocked, maybe. Not shocked because Dad had been out with my language arts teacher, but that neither of them had said anything to me about it. I mean, we were a family, weren't we? If *I* had gone somewhere at night with my teacher, wouldn't I have been expected to tell Dad?

Sitting on my bed, back to the wall, knees drawn up to my chest, I hugged my legs and thought about how all during class that day, Miss Summers had known she was going out with my dad that evening, and hadn't said a word.

I tried to imagine them sitting across from each other in a cozy restaurant. Snuggling up against each other in the car. In the living room of her house, maybe. I didn't let my imagination take it any further. Yeah, I was hurt, I guess.

How long had this been going on? I mean, I invited my teacher to go to a concert with us in December, and seven weeks later she's dating my dad behind my back. Wasn't there a law or something? Boy, I'll bet the principal would like to hear about this, I thought. The superintendent, even. The whole board of education!

There was a light tap on the door, and it opened halfway.

"Al?" came Dad's voice. "May I come in?"

"Yeah," I said finally, in a voice as flat as cardboard.

Dad sat down on one corner of my dresser. "What's the matter? You okay?"

"Nothing, and yes," I said in answer.

"Come on, Al. What is it?"

"I thought we were a family," I told him.

"We are, unless something happened between the time you stalked out of the living room and now."

"I thought families told each other things—what they were going to do and everything."

"Ah." Dad nodded and was quiet for a minute. "You're mad because I didn't tell you that I'd be out this evening with Sylvia. Right?"

Sylvia? They were "Ben and Sylvia" now?

"Right."

"I'm curious, Al. How did you know?"

"Because that's what *she* called me today—a 'symphony in green.' "

"Oh."

"And I'm wondering how many other evenings you were out with her and didn't tell me."

"I didn't realize I needed your permission."

I gave him a look and went on studying my knees. "Whenever *I* go out, you want to know where I'm going, who I'm with, and what I'll be doing. You didn't even tell me you'd be out. You could have been mugged or something, and I'd never have known it."

"You're not mad because you were worried I'd be mugged, Al. Admit it. What I can't understand is that you were so eager to get Sylvia and me together last December, and now that you've succeeded to a certain extent, you're upset."

"What do you mean, 'to a certain extent'?" I shot back.

"Only that I have been seeing your teacher now and then. It isn't as though we were spending every spare minute together."

"Have you had sexual intercourse?" I asked.

"What?"

"Sex, I mean."

"Al!"

"Well?"

"That, young lady, is none of your business."

"You *have,* then!"

"Al, what in the world's got into you? I'm going to answer you this one time, but it's not a question you can ask again. No, we have not."

"Why can't I ask it again?"

"Because it's none of your business."

"You'd ask *me!"*

"Because I'm the dad and you're the daughter. Got it?"

I think I felt better then—that there were some limits, I mean. I guess it just caught me off-guard, Dad dating Miss Summers, and there were a lot of things I wanted to know. It helped to be told there were some kinds of things I could ask about and some I couldn't. Sexual intercourse, I couldn't.

We were both quiet. When I glanced up at Dad again, he was smiling, so I said, "What *can* I ask?"

"You can ask where we went."

"Where did you go?" I tried not to smile, but the corners of my mouth were tugging upward.

"We drove to an Afghan restaurant in Bethesda, browsed through a secondhand bookstore, and went back to her house for coffee."

"Oh." I thought about that, having coffee in Miss Summers's living room. "Have I ever been in that restaurant?"

"No, but I'll be glad to take you sometime."

"What else can I ask?"

"If we had a good time."

"Did you?"

"Yes."

"Can I ask if you're going to see her again?"

"Yes and yes. We seem to get along together okay."

"Just okay?"

Dad raised one eyebrow to let me know I was skating on thin ice again, but he said, "We enjoy each other's company. That's all I know for sure."

"Okay," I said.

Dad went downstairs after that, and now that we'd had it out, I began to feel a little excited about it. Like, wow! Dad dating my language arts teacher! And they'd talked about me, obviously, because how else would Dad have known I was a "symphony in green"?

My first thought was to call Elizabeth or Pamela and tell them, but my second thought was no, better wait, and my third thought was that I was feeling left out—as though things were rushing on ahead of me. Dad and Miss Summers, Les and Marilyn . . . It's strange how you keep hoping for something—like a mother or sister-in-law—and then when you think you're about to get it, you get cold feet.

I was also thinking about sex. I guess you think about that a lot in seventh grade because it keeps jumping out at you—in the words of songs, the unit on Our Changing Bodies, Ann Landers. . . . You look at yourself in the mirror before you get in the tub, and you notice that you really *are* changing. It's scary, weird, and great, all at the same time.

The phone rang about nine-thirty. I wondered if it was Elizabeth again, but this time it was Pamela, and she asked if I wanted to join an earring club. The truth was that at that particular moment I wanted to join anything I possibly could. I wanted to be part of everything that would give me something to hold on to while the world around me tipped out of balance. I wanted to be surrounded by Sisters.

"Come over for a few minutes," Pamela said, so I did.

There were two other girls from school at Pamela's, Karen and Jill. They were both pretty, both popular, Karen a little on the heavy side, Jill thin as a straw. When I saw them there in Pamela's bedroom, I knew I could knock their socks off by telling everyone that Miss Summers was going out with my dad, but I didn't. I wanted so much to be exactly like everyone else that I kept it to myself.

"Here's what I found out," Pamela told me after we'd dug into the bag of peanuts she was passing around. "You know the shop, Tiddly Winks, across from the post office? They've just started an earring club, and here's how it works: If you can get as many as four girls to form a chapter, you get four percent off every time you buy earrings, a percent for every girl in the chapter."

"Alice, you should see their selection!" said Karen. "They've got everything!"

"Why don't we register the whole seventh grade, and then we'd get a hundred percent off?" I asked.

"The limit is five per chapter," Jill said. "But the earrings are cheap. Only five or six dollars a pair."

I was getting an allowance of ten dollars a week, plus whatever I earned at the Melody Inn, but I had to buy my own lunch out of it on days I got cafeteria food.

"Come on, Alice," said Karen. "You don't *have* to buy a lot. All you have to do is go with us to register, then buy at least one pair a month to keep your membership active."

So the next day after school, Pamela and I went with Jill to her locker, then to Karen's.

"Where are you going?" Elizabeth asked when she saw us heading away from the school bus.

"Earring club," I called to her. "Want to go?"

"She can't," said Pamela. "Tiddly Winks carries only pierced earrings. They don't have any clips at all."

"See you!" I said to Elizabeth, and headed down the corridor.

I've never liked shopping with other people, to tell the truth, because I like to go home after I find what I want. When we shopped together, Pamela tried on earrings while the rest of us watched. Then Jill tried on earrings. It took forever. If the other girls were going to buy a pair each week, I would too, but I wondered if I could do this for the next two years of junior high school. One pair of earrings a week for one hundred and four weeks meant one hundred and four pairs of earrings. I should have so many ears! Sisterhood, I told myself.

I went home that evening with a pair of pink ceramic elephants. My earlobes were healing up nicely. I always wore my studs on evenings and weekends, but now that I'd joined the earring club, I could wear a different pair to school each day.

The next day we traded. At noon we got together in the cafeteria and decided what earrings each girl was going to wear the next week, and what clothes would go with the earrings. It was all very "in." Boring, but "in." The trouble was the more "in" I got, the more "out" Elizabeth seemed to be.

"Why don't you just pierce your ears and get it over with?" I asked her. "Then you can join." But she didn't answer. I mean, sometimes all it takes is one little thing to fit in, but Elizabeth just wouldn't do it.

In language arts, I really studied Miss Summers, and I think she knew, because she didn't call on me much at all. It was as though she didn't want to seem to be favoring me. I got out the door as soon as class was over, so I wouldn't be alone with her. That would have been too awkward. If I knew she was really going to marry Dad, that would be different, but what if they drifted apart and broke up, like Les and Marilyn once before? Then it would be really embarrassing. I just hoped that if she and Dad stopped seeing each other, it would be after I was out of her class in June.

On Saturday, though, Lester was out with Marilyn and I'd been over to Pamela's all evening trying on earrings. When I got home, I walked in to find Dad playing the piano and Miss Summers singing. Dad stopped playing and smiled at me.

"Hello, Alice," Miss Summers said.

"Hi." I went right on out to the kitchen as though I often came home to find one of my teachers leaning her elbows on our piano. I got a 7UP and was looking for the cheese when I realized they had it out there, so I had to go back into the living room again.

"Listen, Al," said Dad. "You'll find this interesting, I think. Do you know what piece this is?"

I sat down in the beanbag chair in one corner, taking big swigs of my 7UP. Dad played a few bars of a piece on the piano—five quick notes, one at a time, followed by the last three notes; then another five, and so on.

"Bach," I said.

"That's right, Alice," said Miss Summers, surprised. "How did you know?"

"I can read the title of it from here," I said.

Dad just went on smiling, but he turned around on the piano bench. "Do you know the story of Gounod's 'Ave Maria'?"

I shook my head.

"Well, Gounod wrote a piece that he called 'Meditation,' and someone came along and decided that it would make a perfect melody to accompany Bach's first prelude in *The Well-Tempered Clavier.* Then someone decided that the words to 'Ave Maria' would go perfectly with Gounod's melody. So here we have the bottom part by Bach, the top part by Gounod, and the words to 'Ave Maria.' Listen. . . ."

He looked at Miss Summers and smiled, and she smiled at me. "Excuse my voice, Alice," she said. "I just learned this myself."

Dad started playing those little five-note measures again from the yellow book, and Miss Summers sang 'Ave Maria' along with it. She had a low, soft voice, and she sang easily, not strained or showy. She was leaning her arms on the piano again, and at some point Dad looked up at her and smiled again and she smiled back while she was singing. I liked that—to see Dad smile that way. It was a different smile, and I knew it had been a long time since I'd seen it.

"It's very nice," I said when they finished. What I found interesting was that Dad and Miss Summers were so chummy. I wasn't sure if I was supposed to be in the room or not, upstairs or down. Whether it was proper to talk to Miss Summers about anything except school when you were out of school, and whether I should call her Miss Summers or Sylvia. I felt weird about the whole works, frankly.

So I took my 7UP to my room and realized too late that I'd brought the cheese along with me. When I went back down, Dad and Miss Summers were sitting side by side at the piano. She was playing the upper notes of a song with her right hand, and Dad was playing the base with his left. I couldn't see their other hands. Maybe they were in their laps. Or maybe Dad had his over hers there on the piano bench.

This time I left the room smiling, feeling like Cupid. Here was love hatching in this very house right under my very nose. Maybe.

8

Mar-i-lyn

I HAD this deep-down feeling that Dad might just possibly give Miss Summers an engagement ring on Valentine's Day. The fact that he was crabby made it seem all the more possible: He was probably wrestling with an enormous decision.

If he did propose and she accepted, my whole life would change. I'd go through the rest of junior high as Miss Summers's daughter. She would be here when I had my friends in for overnights, and could make us little sandwiches with the crusts cut off, hot cocoa with whipped cream and cinnamon sticks, and cookies loaded with chocolate chunks, fresh from the oven.

She would teach me how to curl the ends of my hair under and put on panty hose without the legs twisting around three times. When I did something stupid and embarrassing, she'd know the right thing to say; when I was sick, she'd know what to do; and when I was sad, she'd be sad too, because a mom always feels right along with you.

The girls in our earring club spent the next week talking about what to wear on Valentine's Day. We went back to Tiddly Winks and purchased a pair of red ceramic, heart-shaped earrings, a pair of tiny pink cupids, silver cupids, and some gold hearts tied with miniature red bows. Each afternoon we traded off, along with clothes, deciding what we were going to wear to school on Friday, the big day.

"I'm going to wear a white sweater and red pleated skirt," said Karen.

"I'm going to wear my white jeans and a red-and-black shirt," said Jill.

"My mom's going to braid red silk roses in my hair," said Pamela, and they all looked at me. "What are *you* going to wear, Alice?"

"I'll think of something," I told them. What I didn't say was that I usually stick one hand in my closet each morning and pull out whatever it touches first. Then I try to find something to go with it.

Elizabeth hadn't eaten at our table all week, and as we were leaving the cafeteria Thursday, I caught up with her.

"Where've you been?" I asked. "You weren't at our table."

"You've noticed?" she said.

"You're mad," I guessed.

"Not mad. Left out," she told me. "All you and Pamela ever talk about anymore is earrings, earrings, earrings. I'd think you'd get sick of it."

"Well, sometimes I do," I admitted. "What did we used to talk about?" I really couldn't remember.

"Everything. Boys and teachers and life and stuff."

We walked along in silence for a while.

"It's not that we don't like you, Elizabeth. You just don't fit in without earrings. All you'd have to do is—"

"Yes, all *I'd* have to do! Everyone else has to change to fit in with *your* group. *You* don't have to do any changing at all."

She turned at the next corner, just as I was about to ask if I could borrow her red polka-dot shirt to wear the next day.

At home that afternoon, I took everything out of my closet, looking for stuff that was red or pink or white. When Dad got home and came upstairs, my bed was heaped with clothes, and by the time Lester got there, nothing was left in my closet but hangers.

But Lester wasn't interested in what I wore to school on Valentine's Day. He leaned against my doorway and stared off into space like a man who had been hit on the head.

"Les?" Dad said.

Lester moved over toward my window and sat down on the sill. "Well, Dad, it happened," he said.

"You totaled your car?"

"I'm in love."

"I thought this was your monastic period."

"I mean, *really* in love this time."

"You weren't before?" asked Dad. "There was Mar-ilyn, then Crystal, then Marilyn again, and . . ."

"I didn't even know what love was before. This is the original, unexpurgated edition," said Lester. "It's different this time. Everything's different. Even her *name* sounds different. Mar-i-lyn."

"Sounds the same to me," I told him.

"Lester," Dad said, "listen to me. I like Marilyn a lot. I think she is a fantastic young woman. I'd be proud to have her as a daughter-in-law. But I've heard it said, and I think it's true, that it doesn't matter *who* you marry as much as *when* you marry."

"That's ridiculous," said Lester. "Are you saying it wouldn't make any difference if I were to marry Lor-etta Jenkins as long as I married at the right time?"

"Think about it. Under what circumstances would you marry Loretta?"

"If both Marilyn and Crystal ditched me, I flunked out of college, lost all my money, wrecked my car, and had my legs amputated," said Lester.

"That's what I mean," said Dad. "It would be the very worst time to marry anybody."

"But I'm not talking marriage, Dad. Did I mention marriage? Did I say the word *wife*? Did I say *daughter-in-law, mortgage,* or *crabgrass*?"

"Just checking," said Dad.

"Tomorrow's Valentine's Day, Dad, and I want to do something special for Marilyn," Les went on. "I want her to know that this time it's for real—it's love on a higher plane than it was before."

There was the slam of a door outside, and I moved

over to the window to see what Les was looking at.

On the street below, a man was coming around the side of a panel truck carrying a huge bouquet of balloons. There were about seven or eight of the silver Mylar hearts with words like LOVE and ADORABLE YOU on them, and fifteen or so red, white, and pink latex balloons. Altogether, it looked as though the man was in danger of rising.

We didn't say a word. All three of us went downstairs to open the door. All three of us heard the man say, "Delivery for Lester McKinley," and Dad and I watched as Lester signed. When the door closed we stood silently by while Lester opened the little card, which he wordlessly passed to us:

"Crystal," it said.

9

Mayday

WHAT HAD happened, we found out later, was that Crystal Harkins, who plays the clarinet and buys her sheet music at the Melody Inn, heard from Janice Sherman, who heard it from Loretta Jenkins, that Lester McKinley was entering the priesthood.

"Lester is the most unlikely person I can think of to become a priest," Crystal had said, and decided to send him a trial balloon, of sorts, to test him out. But the day the balloons were delivered, we didn't know any of that.

"I can't believe this," Lester was saying after the door closed on the deliveryman. "This cannot be happening." He thrust the balloons at Dad. "Here. They're yours," he bleated.

Dad backed away. "No, you don't, Les. You've got to deal with this somehow."

"Al?" Lester said, offering them to me.

"No way," I told him.

Lester let go of the balloons, and they shot up to the ceiling and bobbed about in one corner of the hallway.

They were still there when I went to school the next morning, dressed in blue jeans, red socks, a white turtleneck, and an old red shirt of Carol's that came down below my knees. There were tiny gold hearts dangling from each ear.

Some days you just know you look good, and that was one of them. Pamela and I sat together on the bus, and she told me that every time I moved my head, my earrings caught the sunlight and gleamed. She had red silk roses woven in her long blond hair, just as she'd said she would, and was wearing a white angora sweater with a necklace of red hearts, and red heart-shaped earrings.

"Valentine girls," Patrick commented approvingly as he passed, and we smiled.

Valentine's Day in seventh grade isn't like February 14 in sixth. Almost nothing in junior high school is the way it was back in elementary, and we didn't have to decorate stupid shoe boxes to hold valentines from Woolworth, either.

The way you know it's Valentine's Day in junior high is the way the eighth- and ninth-grade couples make out in the halls, pressed up against lockers, and are two to a coat outside at lunchtime. The gym was being decorated for the ninth-grade dance that night, but our health class was still on the Our Changing Bodies unit in a room off the gym, so that was all right.

When we walked into the room that day, though, the chart of a woman's reproductive organs had been replaced by a chart showing a man's, and while the other girls giggled, Elizabeth quietly went into shock.

Mrs. Bolino, of course, called off the names of body parts like meats at the supermarket and discussed the anatomy of a testicle the way the instructor in home ec discussed chicken pie. But for Elizabeth, that seemed to make things worse. Elizabeth would have been happier if we had called men's organs Unmentionable One and Unmentionable Two.

After class, because she was still in shock, I told her about how back in the Middle Ages men had little pouches called codpieces in the fronts of their trousers to keep their privates in—to show them off, I guess. Somewhere I'd read that they even stuffed their pouches sometimes to make them look bigger.

"Don't *talk* about it," Elizabeth whispered.

"I'm not making this up," I told her. "It's right there in the dictionary. Anyone can look it up."

"Not me," said Elizabeth.

I stopped right there in the hallway. "Elizabeth," I said, "I hope that the baby your mother is expecting turns out to be a boy and you have to change his diaper every day so that someday you'll get over being such a loon."

"Alice!" Elizabeth looked quickly around her. "People *heard*!"

"It doesn't matter. They already know you're a loon."

"They heard about the baby!"

"So? So your mother's having a baby! Big deal!"

"Shh! You don't have to *tell* everyone! Alice, you're awful!" she said, and fled down the hall.

Valentine's Day was only a few hours old, and already I'd made an enemy.

In language arts, I found myself staring at Miss Summers, and wondered if tonight was the night she would become my mother-to-be. Dad had already told us he'd be home late, possibly very late, so he didn't have to tell me that he was taking Miss Summers somewhere, and might come home an engaged man.

I tried to figure out if her smile was any different—if she'd guessed that Dad was going to propose. She didn't have on valentine colors, but she did have on a gold knit dress with bronze jewelry that made her look like an Egyptian princess or something, and her eyes seemed unusually bright, as though she knew this was a special day. Then I realized I'd been staring at her extra hard, because she suddenly glanced in my direction and gave me a quizzical look. I buried my nose in the book again and went on reading the biography of Lincoln Steffens.

"You look like somebody's valentine," Denise Whitlock told me after class.

Even though she'd bullied me last semester, I figured this was a compliment, so I said, "Thanks." Then I tried to think of something nice to say to her in return. *She* looked like somebody's Mack truck, but I couldn't tell her that.

"I like your shoelaces," I said finally. She had on Day-Glo lime green laces with orange ladybugs on them.

"They're my brother's," she said. "Mine broke."

Oh, well.

World studies was more like a fashion show, and Mr. Hensley just couldn't seem to cope. Jill and Karen are in that class along with Pamela and me, and if Miss Summers had seen us four girls in our red, white, and pink clothes and matching earrings, she would have called us a "symphony in rose" or something. Not only that, but Mark Stedmeister and the Three Handsome Stooges walked in wearing black—black turtlenecks, pants, layered shirts—and our assorted pinks and reds against their blacks made us look like a dance company.

I couldn't believe I was one of the Beautiful People. I mean, here I was, Alice McKinley, looking gorgeous, laughing my tinkling laugh, with my gorgeous white teeth showing through my ruby red lips, and these tiny red ribbons on my earrings highlighting the pink in my cheeks. I sat sideways in my chair, legs crossed, feet in the aisle, and Brian, the handsomest Stooge of all, was rubbing the edge of his foot against one of mine. I didn't even move my foot—just went on smiling my wonderful smile, like a rose all covered with dew, preening herself in her very own bud vase.

It was the first day of school I can ever remember

that went too fast. A photographer from the school paper was roaming the hall when we got out of Hensley's class, and he caught a picture of Pamela and Karen and Jill and me coming through the doorway with some of the boys behind us. I think I was looking over my beautiful shoulder at Brian and smiling my bedazzling smile when the picture was taken.

There were pink-frosted cupcakes in the school cafeteria, and fruit cocktail with slices of pink grapefruit. In Our Changing Bodies class, though it had nothing to do with Valentine's Day, the teacher had a medical diagram on the board showing how a male deposits sperm inside a female's body, and Elizabeth would look at the board for one second, then at her desk for five seconds, then the board, then her desk . . .

Frankly, I felt very grown up on the bus going home. I had actually been in a class where the teacher said words like *ejaculation.* I had looked at my reflection in every mirror I'd passed, in every rest room that day, and every single time I'd looked gorgeous. I was on the threshold of being a mature adult woman, and it felt good.

Nobody was home when I got there, not even the balloons. I figured Lester had taken them out in the backyard and simply let them go. They'd probably be over the Potomac by now—possibly halfway into Virginia.

There were a couple Sara Lee brownies left in the refrigerator, and I wanted to get to them before Lester got there, so I sat down with a glass of milk and savored the taste of chocolate on my tongue. I had just started upstairs to brush my teeth when someone knocked, so I clattered back down and opened the door. There stood Patrick with a two-pound box of Whitman's chocolates, tied with a red bow.

I have never in my life been given candy by a boy except for a few candy bars and four chocolate-covered cherries the day we left sixth grade. And here I was, Alice McKinley, standing at the front door facing a boy with a two-pound box, all for me.

"Patrick!" It's all I could manage.

"Hi," he said. That's all he could say too, I guess.

"You . . . want to come in?" I asked.

Patrick came in and thrust out the box. "Happy Valentine's Day," he said.

"But I . . . I mean, we . . ." We'd stopped being boyfriend and girlfriend last September.

"We decided to be *special* friends, didn't we?" he said. "So I don't see why I can't give you candy."

"But I haven't got anything for *you!*" I protested.

"That's okay," said Patrick.

We went into the living room and I set the box on our coffee table, which takes up most of the floor.

"I hope you like Whitman's," said Patrick, sitting down on the edge of the couch.

"Oh, I do."

Patrick looked around, then interlocked his fingers and wiggled them back and forth a few times. "These are the chocolates with a diagram on the lid to show what's inside each one," he said.

"I know." I couldn't possibly eat one then, not after those brownies.

Patrick leaned back and placed the sole of one shoe on the side of the other. "You looked real nice at school," he said. "I mean, you still do."

"Thanks. I like your sweater," I said, noticing it for the first time. The fact was, I couldn't even remember whether Patrick had been in world studies or not, that's how much attention I'd paid to him.

"You want a Coke or anything?" I asked.

"Umm . . . not a Coke," said Patrick.

"We've only got Coke or Sprite," I told him.

"Nothing to drink," said Patrick.

I was sitting in the chair beside the couch, my feet sticking out in front of me. I realized that my left foot was within inches of Patrick's, and remembered how Brian had rubbed one of his shoes against mine in world studies.

"What are you thinking about?" asked Patrick.

I jerked to attention. "Nothing."

"Yes, you are."

"Feet," I told him.

"Feet?"

"Yeah. You know. Crazy thoughts come into your head sometimes."

"Yeah," said Patrick. Finally he stood up. "Well, I've got to go deliver papers. Enjoy the chocolates, Alice."

"I will," I told him. "Thanks a lot."

I walked him to the door and watched him ride

away on his bike. Then I went back to the living room, picked up the big yellow box with the red ribbon around it, and took it upstairs. I sat down on my bed and held the box in my lap. My very first box of chocolates! I couldn't help smiling.

I'd put the ribbon on my bulletin board, put the chocolates in the bottom drawer of my dresser, and choose a different one every day. Or maybe I'd lie on my bed on a bunch of pillows and eat them while I read magazines, the way they do in the movies. Or maybe I'd get a glass candy dish with a lid and keep some of them there, and whenever I had a visitor, I'd say, "Have a chocolate." Just like my own apartment or something.

The door slammed downstairs, and a few moments later Lester walked by my doorway. When he saw the box of chocolates, he stuck his head inside. "Hey, looks like somebody got a valentine!"

"Patrick gave it to me," I said. "He just left."

"No kidding? Patrick again, huh?" Lester leaned against the door frame. "You going to keep the bow on it?"

"I haven't opened them yet," I said.

Lester stared down at me. "Patrick brought them over and you didn't open the box?"

"No . . ."

"You didn't even offer *him* any, Al?"

My chest got that cold feeling you get when you've swallowed an ice cube. "I . . . I'd just had some brownies, and I wasn't hungry, and . . ."

"But *he* was. Listen, Al, the first lesson of dating is this: When a boy gives a girl candy, it's because *he* wants some."

"But I . . . oh, Lester! I just didn't think!" It all made perfect sense. Of course Patrick didn't want a Coke or Sprite. He wanted a huge milk chocolate creme with a nougat center, that's what.

"Lord, Al, that was really dumb," Lester went on. "If I could give you a gadget that would light up or beep when you were about to do something stupid, I would, but sometimes you just don't use your head."

I was on the verge of tears. "What am I going to *do*?"

"Wait until tomorrow. Then call him up, tell him the box was so beautiful you couldn't bear to open it, but now you want to try some of the candy, and you want him to be here when you do so he can choose the first piece."

A reprieve! At last I'd done something stupid that had an escape hatch. I fell backward on my bed, spread-eagled, glad for a second chance. I had to start thinking about other people more—how somebody else might feel. If I'd been thinking about Patrick instead of myself, I would have figured that out.

I decided to focus on Lester and *his* problems. "What are you going to do about Crystal?" I asked.

Lester had gone into the bathroom and I could hear the clink of his cup as he turned on the water. "I don't know what I'm going to do about her, but I can tell you what I did with her balloons. I took them over to Marilyn's and tied them to her door handle, with a note from me. She'll have them by the time we go out tonight."

I bolted straight up, and the chocolates slid off onto the bed. "Lester, no! You didn't!" I jumped to my feet and went out into the hallway.

Lester came to the door of the bathroom, holding the plastic cup. "Of course I did. What's the matter with it?"

"Lester! Those balloons! Didn't you see? One of them read YOU GORGEOUS HUNK."

The water dropped from Lester's hands and spilled all over the rug.

"You're kidding."

"I'm not!"

"I thought they said LOVE. I'm *sure* they said LOVE."

"The Mylar hearts had LOVE on one side but messages on the other, and one of them said YOU GORGEOUS HUNK."

Lester leaned his forehead against the wall and his shoulders slumped.

"Lester," I said quietly, "If I could give you a gadget that would light up or beep when you were about to do something stupid, I would, but sometimes you just don't use your head."

What happened next was that Lester and I rode over to Marilyn's. He was going to park around the corner, and if the balloons were still there, I was to sneak up on the porch and untie the whole bunch, sending them off into oblivion. Too late. The balloons were gone. We went back home, and Lester prepared for his date with Marilyn like he was going off to war.

But what was even worse, Dad came home around ten looking as if he'd just been through one. He didn't say a word—just went out to the kitchen, plugged in the leftover coffee, and slumped down in a chair, waiting for it to heat.

I finally came in and sat beside him.

"Tired?" I said.

"Very."

"Disappointed?"

"Should I be?" he asked.

"Dad, what happened? You can tell me," I said. "Did she say no?"

"Did who say what?"

"M-Miss Summers. Did she . . . ?"

"What does Syliva have to do with anything? I've been doing inventory at the store, Alice, and I'm bone-weary. Even my brains hurt."

"Oh," I said.

I went upstairs and sat looking at the box of chocolates on my bed—the chocolates I never offered to Patrick. I thought of Lester out with Marilyn somewhere, and wondered if they were even speaking. And of Miss Summers, home alone on Valentine's Day when Dad should have been over there proposing.

I felt as though we were all going down in a boat at sea. I wanted to run to the window, fling it open, and shout, "Mayday! Mayday!" That's what they should have called February 14 in the first place.

10

Modern Love

I GUESS if I learned one thing over the weekend, it was that only death is final, because three things happened to prove that Valentine's Day wasn't a total disaster.

Number one: Lester told Marilyn on their date Friday night exactly how he had got the balloons and what he had done with them. Then he and Marilyn went out in her backyard and released the balloons together. Lester said it would have been perfect if Marilyn hadn't said, as the balloons sailed away, "There goes Crystal Harkins forever." *Forever,* Lester told me later, is an awfully long time.

Number two: Dad took Miss Summers to the theater on Saturday night. I know it was a valentine celebration of sorts, because Dad was wearing a bright red tie, which he usually saves for Christmas. Just after he put on his coat, he reached up on the closet shelf for a little box wrapped in red and silver and then went out the door. My heart beat double time. Adults, I guess, can celebrate Valentine's Day whenever they like.

Number three: While Lester was at the Maytag store where he sells washing machines on weekends, and after I'd put in my three hours at the Melody Inn, I came home and called Patrick.

"Patrick," I said, "that box of chocolates you gave me was so pretty I just couldn't open it. But now I'm ready to take the bow off, and I wondered if you'd like to come over and choose the first piece."

"Be right there," said Patrick, and in two minutes he was at the front door.

It was weird doing the same thing all over again, only this time doing it right.

"Hi," he said.

"Come on in," I told him, and we walked into the living room, sat down on the couch, untied the ribbon on the chocolates, and opened the box.

It got easier after that. We read the diagram, found the right shapes, peeked under the cardboard to see what the second layer looked like, exchanged some of the first layer for part of the second, and had three chocolates apiece.

"If I'd known you weren't going to open them till today, I would have waited and bought the box this morning," Patrick said.

"Why?"

"Because valentine candy is half-price now. I could have bought two boxes for what this one cost."

It felt good to hear Patrick say something dumb for a change. To know that the boy who had traveled all over the world with his parents and could count in Japanese could still say the wrong thing.

"That's okay," I told him. "If I had two boxes, I'd get fat."

"I didn't say I'd give them both to you," Patrick said.

Bingo. Two stupid remarks in one day.

The nice thing was that Patrick didn't try to kiss me. We talked about which chocolates we liked best, and Patrick said when he was little he used to lick all the chocolate off each piece and leave the center. When it was time for him to go, I asked if he wanted to take some with him, and he took a whole handful! Then he felt embarrassed, I guess, because he put two back, but they already had dents in them.

"See you Monday," I said as he went outside. "Thanks again." Patrick the Perfect wasn't so perfect after all.

Wouldn't you know, though, that after he left and I was home by myself, Crystal Harkins called.

"Hi, Alice," she said. "How are you?"

"Uh . . . fine, Crystal!" I said. I started to say I hadn't seen her since the *Messiah* concert, but decided that that was the problem exactly.

"Did you have a nice Christmas?" she asked.

"The usual. We went to a Mexican restaurant," I answered.

"That's good," said Crystal.

There was a three- or four-second silence, and then she asked, "Is Les around?"

"He's working today," I told her.

"Oh," said Crystal. Another silence. Then, "Does he have any plans for tonight, would you know?"

"I really don't."

"Did he . . . ?" She laughed a little, as though it were unimportant. "Did he get my balloons?"

"Yeah. That was nice of you, Crystal."

"What did he do with them?"

"I—I'm not sure."

"You're not sure?"

"N-Not exactly."

"Well, are they there? In his room or something?"

"I don't think so, but they could be." It was February but there was sweat running down my back. Here was a problem about Sisterhood I hadn't expected. How could I look out for Marilyn and Crystal both?

"Alice," said Crystal, and her voice was soft. "You really don't have to lie to me." And then she got louder: "What happened to those *balloons*?"

I swallowed. "He and Marilyn let them go."

"He and *Marilyn*?"

I gulped again. "Over in her backyard."

As soon as I'd said, "Marilyn," I knew I shouldn't have, but if I'd said that Lester did it alone, it would have sounded as though he'd been really angry about the balloons, while if I mentioned Marilyn, it might seem as though she'd talked him into it, yet . . .

"Alice," Crystal said, "would you get a piece of paper and take a message to Lester? I want you to write it down, because I want him to get every word."

"Sure," I said. I went to the dining room, tore a sheet of paper out of my notebook, and came back.

"Okay," I told her.

"This is going to take a while, because I'm composing as I go, but write his name down on your paper vertically—you know, *L* at the top, then on the next line, *e*, and so on."

I wrote it like she said.

"Beside the *L*," said Crystal, "write *lousy*." She waited. "Beside the *e*, write *egotistical*."

I began to get the drift.

"Beside the *s* write *stupid*."

By the time we got to the last letter, she had added *thankless*, *extraneous*, and *repugnant*." I didn't know what *extraneous* meant, but I knew it wasn't a compliment. Surprisingly, however, her voice was soft again when she finished.

"After you give that to Lester," she directed, "you can tell him, for me, that I didn't really believe it when I heard he might enter the priesthood, but I think he should reconsider, because I can't think of a better place for him. It might keep him from hurting anyone else."

"Crystal," I said, and my voice was soft too. More like a squeak, actually. "How has Lester hurt you?"

This was a secret of womanhood I just had to know.

She sighed—a long, painful sigh. "By making me believe, when I was with him, that I was the only woman in the world—that he worshiped me. When Lester talks, he looks you right in the eyes, hangs on to every word you say. And the way he kisses . . . Oh, Alice, if he's not locked up, he should be."

After we'd finished talking, I stared down at the notepaper on my lap. If Lester worshiped you and hung on to your every word and was a great kisser, how could he be lousy, egotistical, stupid, thankless, extraneous, and repugnant all at the same time?

Nevertheless, when Lester came home, I offered him some chocolates first to fortify him, then gave him Crystal's message.

"Lester, I'm *sorry!*" I said. "Really! I didn't know what to say! She kept quizzing me, and I just blurted out Marilyn's name. I didn't mean to get you in trouble." What was I *doing*? I was supposed to be sticking up for Sisterhood and I was apologizing to my brother!

You know what he did? Lester went right to the phone, called the florist, and asked him to deliver a rose to Crystal. One single long-stemmed rose, with only his name attached. And then I knew why girls fell for my brother.

I sat on the stairs and listened and watched, and realized I was witnessing modern love in the making. I didn't have to buy any of those romance magazines. I imagined how Crystal would feel, after all that, when she got a single red rose. How could he be repugnant and do that? But how could he love Marilyn with a love that was the true, unexpurgated edition if he was sending a rose to Crystal?

On Sunday, I didn't get one glimmer out of Dad as to how his date with Miss Summers went. I hung around the breakfast table all the while he ate his Wheat Chex, put the milk away for him when he was through, put the dishes in the sink. . . .

"Have a good time last night, Dad?" I asked finally.

"Mmm," he said, not even looking up from his paper.

"She look nice?" I quizzed.

"Mmm," he said again.

I knew I wasn't going to get one bit of information out of him, so I went upstairs.

In language arts the next day, the first thing I looked for when I entered the classroom was Miss Summers's left hand, to see if she was wearing a diamond. I tried to think what I should do if she was—rush over and hug her? Say, "Mother!"? Or would she hug me after class and tell me the news herself?

I gave her a big smile as I walked past her desk, and she smiled back. She was wearing beige this time, with a sweater of blue, green, and rust. But she had the attendance book open, and her left hand was beneath it, so I couldn't really see anything.

When she'd taken attendance, she started talking about some of the great biographers of the world, and how they went about their work. Now she had her hands folded in front of her. I could see her left hand, but not her ring finger. I cocked my head a little to the right to see around one thumb.

"What do you think, class? Is it possible to write a completely objective biography of someone, or are your own prejudices going to sneak in undetected? Let's have some examples here."

Hands shot up—all hands except Miss Summers's. She had unhooked her fingers now, but her left hand was lying loosely on the desk top, turned on its side, and I still couldn't see her ring finger. I leaned farther out into the aisle, trying to get a glimpse of something shiny.

And suddenly I was conscious of a silence in the room, then a giggle, and realized that Miss Summers was looking right at me. "You look terribly uncomfortable, Alice," she said.

I bolted upright. "I'm fine," I said, but I wasn't, because when Miss Summers moved her hand at last, I saw that the ring finger was absolutely naked, and a dull rush of disappointment came over me. Dad was dragging his feet, Miss Summers would get away, and there was nothing, absolutely nothing, I could do about it.

In world studies, though, things were different. Jill and Karen had got together over the weekend and made up a list of couples. There just happened to be eleven boys in Mr. Hensley's class, and eleven girls, so Jill and Karen had divided the list of students into couples, just for fun. They taped it up on the blackboard in one corner and titled it "Famous Couples in History." Mr. Hensley looked at it as though it were some undecipherable message from outer space and let it be. But most of the kids were grinning.

Pamela was matched up with Mark Stedmeister, of course, and Jill, Karen, and I were matched up with the Three Handsome Stooges. There was my name beside Brian's.

Alice and Brian, it said! I couldn't believe I had only been in junior high for five months, and already my name was being mentioned in the same breath with the most handsome guy in seventh grade—a jerk, but handsome. I couldn't help smiling a little bit. I mean, the eight of us had become sort of a clique now. We didn't eat lunch together or go walking around the neighborhood the way Pamela and Elizabeth and I used to do with Mark, Tom Perona, and Patrick. But we horsed around a lot before and after class, and teased each other in the halls. I wondered if the eight of us would hang around together in eighth too, and if we'd all go to the ninth-grade dance together.

Brian sat right behind me, and he thrust his feet under my chair, rubbing the back of my shoes with the toes of his Adidas sneakers. He took a ruler and ran it up and down my spine, making me shiver, then laugh. When Hensley wasn't looking, he took the ruler and tapped each of my ceramic banjo-shaped earrings, making a sort of *ping*.

I was so excited about being one of the Famous

Eight that it wasn't until halfway through the period that I realized Patrick must have been matched with someone too, and finally, when we were taking a true-and-false quiz, I went to the pencil sharpener just so I could see whose name was there beside Patrick's.

It was a girl named Sara, and after I went back to my seat, I turned slightly and stared at the girl down at the end of the row behind me. She had dark hair like Elizabeth's. She wasn't gorgeous, wasn't ugly, wasn't fat or thin or tall or short. Just sort of average and quiet, but somehow—without knowing why—I felt jealous.

Why had they put Sara's name with Patrick's? Had he taken *her* chocolates too? Did he like her? Did she like him? What did I know about Sara? Nothing, and that made her all the more mysterious.

"Time!" called Mr. Hensley. "Turn your papers in, please!"

I stared. I'd only answered two questions. Papers were being passed shoulder over shoulder to the front of the room, and when the bell rang that day, I went out in the hall with Brian tickling me from behind, and Pamela and Mark Stedmeister holding hands. Jill and Karen were flirting with the other two Stooges. My own lips were smiling and my mouth was laughing, and Brian was trying to find all the places where I was ticklish. I could tell by the looks on some of the other faces that we were envied. The Beautiful People. Now that I had "arrived," however, it was like opening a gorgeous box and finding nothing inside.

I was still thinking about boxes when I got home, and at dinner I asked Dad, "What was in that little box you gave Miss Summers?"

Dad slowly ladled out the meat and potatoes into a big bowl. "I wasn't aware I was being watched."

"I just happened to notice," I told him.

"It truly is none of your business, Al," he said, "but the fact of the matter is, I gave her a Vivaldi cassette."

I stared. "Valentine's Day, and you gave her a cassette?"

"Yes, and she loved it. Do you have a problem with that?"

I had a problem with that. I had a problem with everything. I had a problem with Brian and Patrick and Pamela and Jill and Karen and Elizabeth and Crystal and Marilyn, but most of all I was having a problem with myself.

11

Wonder Woman

LIFE, I'VE decided, is holding your breath to see what happens next. And what happened next was that there was a sign-up sheet outside the cafeteria for students who wanted to be in the junior high talent show.

Going up onstage in front of three hundred kids and putting your life on the line is not something that would have occurred to me for one moment. I mean, if somebody had said, "Al, take your choice: Swim across this crocodile-infested river or do something for the talent show," I'd probably have taken the river. But every kid in the All-Stars Fan Club was involved in the show, every girl in our earring club was talking about what kind of an act she was going to do, and they just assumed that I, naturally, was going to be in it. I, naturally, assumed that I was going to sit in the audience and clap.

"What are you going to do, Alice?" Karen asked as we sat on Pamela's bed, each trying on the others' earrings and passing them on.

"Do?"

"In the talent show! Tomorrow's the last day to sign up. The list has been there for a month."

"I—I don't know," I stammered.

"Dress rehearsal's only a week away," Pamela reminded me.

"Just put your name on the sign-up sheet, and you can decide later," said Jill. "But I've got just the costume for you. I wore it last year for a dance recital, and it'll be perfect on you: Wonder Woman."

I stared. "But what would I *do*?"

Jill shrugged. "I don't know. But it's a wonderful costume, and you could think of something. Can you dance?"

I shook my head.

"Sing?"

"Are you kidding?"

Pamela nodded. "Trust me: She can't."

My lack of singing ability was notorious. I can play simple songs on the piano, but I've never been able to carry a tune. I can't even tell if the notes go up or down.

"How about juggling?" asked Karen.

"Forget it."

Jill sighed and handed me some loop earrings with little beads on them. "Well, it would be a shame to let the costume go to waste."

I walked home from Pamela's later, my breath mak-

ing clouds of steam in front of my face, and found
Lester working out in his sweats in the basement. He
has a bench down there that looks like a torture cham-
ber, and he lifts weights until the whole place smells
like feet.

In case you don't know much about bodybuilding,
the aim is to make your muscles and veins so big that
eventually all your insides show up on the outside.
You can even point out the liver, stomach, and spleen
without a chart.

I sat down on the stairs and listened to Lester
grunt. When he'd finished one set, I said, "Lester, I've
got to sign up for the talent show by tomorrow, and
Jill's got a Wonder Woman costume for me, but I can't
think of anything to do."

Lester lay there panting. "You could always walk
out onstage with your arms full of Wonder bread and
throw slices to the audience."

"*Think*, Lester!"

"Okay. How about going three days without food,
then walking onstage with your arms full of Wonder
bread and eating it all yourself? You'd even have the
audience counting slices as you wolfed them down.
'Fifteen . . . sixteen . . . seventeen . . .'"

I stormed out of the basement and cornered Dad
that evening as he was scraping carrots and potatoes
at the sink.

"What could I do in the school talent show, wearing a Wonder Woman costume?" I asked.

I can tell by the way Dad's shoulders stiffen that

being a single parent just gets too much for him some-times.

"Hey, it's okay," I told him. "I know it's my prob-lem, but just brainstorm. Think of anything at all." He *had* to come up with something better than Wonder bread.

Dad went on scraping. "Refresh my memory, Al. Wonder Woman wears a stars-and-stripes costume, doesn't she?"

"Yes . . ."

"Well, why don't you walk onstage holding the American flag and lip-synch "The Star-Spangled Ban-ner" or something? That's cool, isn't it?"

Why is it that when parents think they're with it, they're so totally out of it?

"Think of something else," I said.

"Okay. Find some guys who are willing to wear Superman costumes, and then all of you form a pyra-mid, with Wonder Woman at the top."

When I made a face, Dad said, "Well, use your head, Al. There must be something you can do to entertain, instruct, or otherwise amuse your friends."

I leaned over the sink and pretended to vomit. It occurred to me that that's all I knew how to do. "I could always go onstage and barf," I said.

"Fine. It's settled, then," said Dad.

That night, I called Carol's apartment in Chicago, and out of desperation, when she didn't answer, I di-aled Aunt Sally. "Any ideas at all," I told her.

"Well, let me see," said Aunt Sally. "I remember being in a talent show once. I don't know if it was junior high or high school, but I do remember that I recited Joyce Kilmer's 'Trees.' I think a friend was playing the music in the background."

I closed my eyes.

"But a *Wonder* Woman costume?" She was quiet for a moment. "Why don't you do a skit, dear?"

"A skit?"

"Yes. Like a little play. You could do an antidrug skit. Have a bunch of kids sitting around pretending to sniff glue out of a paper bag, and then Wonder Woman, with your school's name on her chest, bursts into the room and grabs the bag."

"Aunt Sally, is Carol at your house by chance?" I asked.

"No, dear, but Milt's here, and he has an idea."

I held my breath as my uncle came on the line.

"Alice, honey, do you have a trapdoor on your stage?"

"I don't think so."

"Well, if you do, see, you come on carrying a bag with a false bottom. Set that down over the trapdoor, and get somebody underneath passing things up through it, and there you are, taking out twenty-five rabbits or something, and that'd be a real hit, I tell you."

"Thanks, but we don't have either a trapdoor or rabbits," I told him.

I went upstairs and lay on my stomach. The thing about life is that somehow you manage to ruin all the stuff that's fun. I could have a wonderful time at the talent show if I was just sitting in the audience.

It wasn't as though we were the Rockettes, I told myself, all performing together. Why didn't I just say, "Great! You guys be in the show and I'll cheer like crazy"? I don't know. I didn't want my friends doing anything without me. Whatever the Sisters did, I'd do too, even if we made complete fools of ourselves. So here I was, all dressed up like Wonder Woman, with no ideas whatsoever.

The more I thought about Uncle Milt's suggestion, though, the more I thought about magic tricks, and I finally decided to come onstage dressed as Wonder Woman and do a wonderful trick. I didn't know exactly what I'd do yet, but there was an old magic book of Lester's in the basement, so I leafed through it and found a hat trick. I would take my Wonder Woman hat, sew a false bottom in it, the way it showed in the book, then fold up a ten-foot scarf inside a slit in the fake bottom.

I called Jill and told her about it, and she said she would teach me a simple soft-shoe routine so that I could dance onstage to a tune from *Guys and Dolls*. Then I'd show the audience the inside of my hat to prove it was empty, whirl around a couple times, put my fingers in the hat, and pull out a ten-foot scarf from the slit at the bottom. Exit with scarf wrapped loosely around me, to wild applause.

Jill came over. The problem was that Wonder Woman's headpiece wasn't big enough, so we had to use a black top hat, but it looked okay. Putting the scarf inside the fake bottom was easy. Getting the Wonder Woman costume to look like it belonged on my body was not. My boobs weren't big enough to hold the top up (Jill's are enormous for a seventh grader, even though she's skinny!), so Jill sewed some straps over the shoulders. The hips were a little tight, but the boots were loose at the tops, not skintight the way Wonder Woman was supposed to wear them. They would do, though.

We spent every afternoon for a week rehearsing the dance step in our basement, and I finally decided I could at least get through it without falling on my face. At the dress rehearsal, I was sandwiched between Elizabeth, who was doing a dance from the *Nutcracker,* and a boy who played the piccolo while his cat wailed along with it. Most of the performers were either seventh graders who didn't know how bad they were, or ninth graders who were really, really good. Patrick was one of the seventh graders who didn't embarrass himself; he had a drum solo.

The day of the performance, I felt queasy, so I didn't eat any breakfast. Then I was afraid I'd be sick *because* I hadn't eaten breakfast, so I pigged out at lunch. By the time I went backstage in my Wonder Woman costume, the top held up by straps, the shorts too tight, the boots too loose, all I could think about was getting through the performance without my knees giving way.

Patrick, two acts ahead of me, got an encore, and played a second number. Then it was Elizabeth in her white tutu and her gorgeous dark hair and eyelashes, and finally, my heart beating double time, I heard my cue—the music from *Guys and Dolls*—and I soft-shoed my way onstage. I felt a little stiff and realized I wasn't smiling at all, but nobody laughed or booed, so I began to limber up, and I was really pleased that I didn't have any trouble getting the ten-foot scarf out of the hat. I even heard a little applause when the whole scarf was out. I was whirling it around, letting it fall loosely around me, when I felt a sudden tug at the other end.

I looked down and saw the cat, from the next act, pouncing on the end of my scarf. The kids started laughing. The boy who owned the cat was on his hands and knees backstage, hissing the cat's name, but the stupid thing paid no attention at all.

Here's the difference between a seventh and a ninth grader, as I figured it out later. If I had been a ninth grader, I would have laughed along with the audience, picked the cat up in my arms, done a few steps more, then bowed, as if it were all a part of the act.

Instead, I froze, then tugged at the scarf, then glared at the boy backstage, and finally walked off, my face burning, dragging the scarf and the cat behind me, to wild laughter from the audience.

I think I knew how Pamela must have felt back in sixth grade when I grabbed her hair onstage. I felt as though all the sins I had ever committed had come back to haunt me in those four or five seconds it took me to make my exit.

It was all I could do to keep from crying.

"Life's rough, kid," a ninth-grade boy said as I walked past him, swallowing and swallowing.

"Things like that happen to everybody sometime," said Patrick. "You did okay, though, Alice. Really."

Patrick's always there for me; I almost wished we were going together again, but I couldn't think of anything else at the moment except how bad I felt. I would never be in another talent show as long as I lived. Why had I done it? Whose life was this, anyway?

A ninth-grade singer got first prize, and Patrick got second. If the prizes had gone on and on, I might have gotten twenty-fifth or twenty-sixth.

"Well, you don't have to be *mad,* Alice," Jill said as I thrust the costume in her hands after the show. "We didn't *force* you to be in it."

"I know. I'm only mad at myself."

"Oh, forget it. Everybody else has," Karen told me.

She was right, in a way. I remember something that Mrs. Plotkin, my sixth-grade teacher, told me once: "If you worry a lot about what other people think of you, it might surprise you to know how little they think about you at all."

And when I told Lester what had happened, he said, "You know what, Al? They loved it. And you know why? Because they were so glad it was happening to you and not to them."

12

Snow

IT HELPED to think that as I was up in my room that afternoon agonizing over what had happened at the talent show, Crystal Harkins might be in her room crying her eyes out over Lester. The Suffering Sisters of the Sisterhood or something. I wondered if there were groups of boys somewhere exploring their deepest feelings about love and girls and life in general. Somehow I didn't think so.

I figure that in the twelve years I've been alive, about thirty-two really awful, humiliating, ridiculous things have happened to me—all of them when I was above the age of four, which is the furthest back I can remember. And who can tell how many embarrassing things happened when I was in diapers that I don't know about at all! But if thirty-two things happened to me in the nine years I can remember, that's four terrible things per year. Which means that if I live to be eighty, I have 272 really awful, humiliating, ridiculous things yet to happen in my life. I don't think I can stand this.

I used to wish that anyone who had seen me do something stupid would just sort of disappear. Evaporate. When I'd learn that a relative had died, and it was someone who had watched me do something embarrassing, I couldn't help but feel a guilty sense of relief that he was gone and had taken the memory with him. But there was no way I could vaporize all three hundred kids who had been sitting in the school auditorium during the talent show. That was something I'd have to live with.

"If I could just think of a way to fend them off," I said to Lester, when I told him about the 272 horrible things yet to come.

"You can't, Al," he said, "but you could always go around with a paper bag over your head so you wouldn't have to look anyone in the face."

I couldn't help noticing that, despite the joking, his voice was surprisingly gentle, as though he really, truly cared. There had been a change in him lately, and even Dad noticed.

"Al," Dad said that evening as we were doing the laundry in the basement, separating the clothes into white, colored, and hopelessly dirty. Lester was out with Marilyn, so we had to sort his clothes for him. All of Lester's clothes go in the "hopelessly dirty" pile. "Does Lester seem different to you?"

I nodded. "Ever since Marilyn came back in the picture."

"That's what I was thinking. Much as I hate to see Lester seriously involved with anyone at his age, I have to admit that she's been a good influence on him."

I was curious. "Why do you hate to see him involved? What are you afraid will happen?"

"Oh, all kinds of things. He could decide to marry before he's through college, he could marry just because Marilyn wants to. . . ."

"But once he's married, Dad, you could stop worrying about him, couldn't you?"

Dad looked over at me, his arms full of clothes. "Al, you don't understand one thing about parenthood," he said.

The next day, Mr. Hensley announced a different sort of assignment. Right in the middle of our study of Asia, he suddenly started talking about all the great names in history—Confucius, Gandhi, George Washington, Lincoln. . . .

"Every February," he said, facing the class in his old gray suit and navy blue tie, "I ask my students to take a look at historical figures and see if they can determine some of the characteristics common to all famous men and women. I don't expect you to spend hours and hours on this, and you can limit your research to encyclopedias if you like. But see what you can come up with. The paper will be due a week from today."

It was a better assignment than "Identify the impact of foreign influence on the development of the Indian subcontinent" or "Explain the historical basis of conflicts in the Middle East." It was sort of interesting, in fact, because there wasn't just one right answer. I always loved tests with essay questions, so you could write around them.

When I got home that afternoon, I took a bag of potato chips, a banana, and five volumes of our encyclopedia, and sprawled on the dining-room floor beside the bookshelves. I just leafed through the pages, and every time I came across a famous name, I wrote it down and read the article.

Lester came home from the university and sat down in the beanbag chair in the living room, with a Sprite.

"Master's thesis?" he asked, looking at all the books around me.

"I'm supposed to find the common characteristics of great men and women," I said. "So far they're not alike at all. I've looked up Einstein and Lincoln and Helen Keller and Florence Nightingale, and they're all different."

"All you have to do is write down the ways they're alike?" asked Lester. "Piece of cake! You don't even need the encyclopedia, Al."

"How?" I asked.

"Well, you can write that they each had two parents."

"Lester . . ."

"They were all born without significant brain damage."

I stretched out on my stomach with my arms up over my head.

"None of them died in infancy," Lester continued. "See, Al, you make too much work out of things."

After he went upstairs, I lay there wondering if Einstein ever lay on his stomach in the dining room, working on an assignment. If Florence Nightingale had an older brother. If Gandhi ever in his life ate a potato chip, and at what point in your life you knew you were destined for greatness. I mean, did these people suspect, when they were twelve going on thirteen, that their names would be in an encyclopedia someday?

I was still there, eating potato chips, when Dad came in, and he stumbled over one of my books.

"Darn it, Al, do you have to take up half the floor?" he barked. "Look at this mess! Books all over the place, a banana peel . . . You've got ten seconds to get it up off the floor, and I mean *now*."

I looked at Dad, then around at the books. If anybody had expected Henry Ford or the Wright brothers to be famous when they were grown, don't you suppose they would have been treated with a little more respect? If people had known that Lincoln would be president, wouldn't somebody have given him a better job than splitting logs?

"Dad," I said, "just remember that the kid you kick around may own your bank someday. The daughter you scold may be your senator somewhere down the line."

Dad just stood there, his head cocked to one side. "And if it wasn't for *me,*" he said, "you wouldn't be sitting here on the floor at all with one hand in the potato chips. Now *move* it!"

I'm not sure what it was, but I just felt out of sorts—ready to argue at the drop of a hat. I hadn't been to Elizabeth's for several weeks. I was sick of the All-Stars Fan Club. After that letter to Izzy, I'd concentrated on writing letters to authors and waiting for replies, but one of them wrote:

> Dear Alice:
>
> I'm glad you liked my book, but your letter has the ring of a school assignment or, at the very least, a put-up job. Why don't you spend your time writing something you'd really enjoy?

Bingo! I thought. Weekends, of course, were taken up with the earring club. Karen and Jill didn't sleep over, but we met at Pamela's on Fridays to decide what we were going to buy on Saturdays, and then we went over to Jill's or Karen's on Sundays to try on what we'd bought. B-O-R-I-N-G.

Other people's lives seemed to be going all right, so I didn't know what it was about mine. Something was obviously going on between Dad and Miss Summers; Janice Sherman at the Melody Inn, who used to have a crush on Dad, was dating an oboe instructor now, and Dad was very, very happy that she had given up on him; Crystal, after receiving Lester's rose, had called him up, sobbing, and Lester had gone over to cheer her up; Patrick, as far as I could tell, got along perfectly fine without me. Which left me with Pamela, Jill, Karen, Mark Stedmeister, and the Three Handsome Stooges.

This might not have been so bad if we'd done something interesting. I mean, I really liked being one of the Beautiful People. There isn't any law against being popular; it was fun having other kids look up to us, thinking we had something special. But the fact is, we didn't. We just happened to get paired up on that silly "Famous Couples of History" list, and things sort of snowballed from there. All the Stooges did was tease and tickle us, and all the girls did was laugh, and after a while, when everything ticklish had been tickled and you've laughed all your different laughs, you think, Is this all there is to seventh grade?

I made a point of sitting with Elizabeth the next morning on the bus.

"Why don't you come over tonight?" I asked her.

"You always go to Pamela's on Fridays," she answered.

"Well, I won't this time. Come on over and we'll spy on Lester." I was really scraping the bottom of the barrel.

"I already told my aunt I'd spend the night there," she said.

"What do you do at your aunt's?"

Elizabeth shrugged. "Play cards. Make milk shakes. Read mysteries aloud to each other—stuff like that."

All at once I wanted to visit Elizabeth's aunt and play cards and make milk shakes and read mysteries out loud. A lot more than I wanted to try on earrings with Pamela, Karen, and Jill. But I hadn't been invited.

It started to snow around lunchtime. Light flakes at first, then heavier and heavier, and the rumor went around that we were getting off early.

In Maryland, everyone goes nuts when it snows. When snow is forecast in Maryland, people rush to the store to buy fifty pounds of hamburger so they won't starve if they're snowbound for a day or two. With only a half-inch of snow on the ground, cars plow into each other, trucks stall, buses skid, and traffic is tied up for two miles on the beltway. And when snow comes unexpectedly, even the federal government closes down and everyone goes home except the president. All he has to do is walk upstairs.

We all cheered when we saw the yellow buses pulling up an hour early. Everyone was shouting and laughing as we ran to our lockers and got our stuff. When we went outside, guys started pelting girls with snowballs. Brian came up, pulled open the neck of my coat, and stuffed a snowball down the inside of my yellow turtleneck. I shrieked, of course, because everyone else was laughing, but the truth was, I was a little sick of Brian right then.

Lester was already home when I got there, and Dad arrived shortly afterward. The snow was really coming down then, and the radio was talking about the number of accidents in the area.

"I figured we wouldn't have many customers anyway, so I decided to close up shop," Dad said. "How about if we make soup?"

Lester and I didn't exactly jump up and down, because we know Dad's recipe for soup: two cans of chicken broth, one can of V-8, and all the leftovers he can find in the refrigerator, simmered for two hours. This wouldn't be so bad if he stuck to meat and vegetables. But Lester swears he found some oatmeal floating around on the top of his soup once, and I know for a fact that Dad once scraped off the peanut butter from a half-eaten sandwich and added that to the kettle.

Dad was just starting for the kitchen when someone rang the doorbell and Lester went to answer. He opened the door and in walked Loretta Jenkins. She didn't even wait to be asked. She just stood there in the hallway with snow all over her hair and the shoulders of her coat, and reminded me of the angel Gabriel, come to tell Mary she was pregnant.

"Hi," she said, looking right into Lester's eyes. If she knew Dad and I were there, she didn't say anything.

"Hello," Lester said, taking a step backward.

"I'm off to make some soup," Dad said, escaping to the kitchen.

I didn't offer to help, because I really wanted to hear what Loretta was going to say, so I went over to the beanbag chair in the living room and turned the TV on low.

"I guess you decided against the priesthood, huh?" Loretta said, getting right to the point.

"What?" Lester stared.

"I saw you with Marilyn Rawley last week," Loretta said, "and I heard that Crystal Harkins sent you some balloons. She told me."

Lester blinked.

"Lester," said Loretta, "I'm going to come right out and say this. I've liked you for a long time, though I don't suppose you've noticed. But I'm a woman of the nineties now, and a nineties woman isn't afraid to go after what she wants. If Marilyn and Crystal are in the running, you can count me in."

For once in his life, Lester was speechless.

"I'm inviting you out on Saturday night—a little party with some friends of mine," Loretta said.

Lester thrust his hands in his pockets. "Loretta," he said, "we've got to talk."

"Fine."

"I'm serious about Marilyn Rawley. I can't help it."

"And I'm serious about you; I can't help that, either."

"What I'm trying to tell you—"

"Look. Do we have to talk here?" Loretta asked. "Can't we at least walk around the block?"

"Okay," Lester said. "I'll get my jacket."

I followed him upstairs. "Lester, don't go," I warned, throwing Sisterhood to the winds. "You know what happened when you went for a walk with Marilyn."

"Don't worry," Lester said. "Loretta couldn't get a rise out of me if she had ten boobs on her body."

"You're going to get her hopes up."

"I can handle this," said Lester. He slipped on his jacket.

But I wasn't so sure. "Thirty minutes, and I'll send the Saint Bernard," I told him as he clattered downstairs.

As it happened, he was back in fifteen. I came down to find him sitting in the kitchen, slicing onions for Dad. Already the smell of chicken broth and V-8 filled the kitchen, as well as something else I couldn't name—sauerkraut, maybe, left over from a week ago Tuesday.

"Well, are you going to Loretta's party?" I asked him.

"I am not," said Lester.

"You're off the hook, then?"

"Not exactly."

"What did she say?"

"That if I'm playing the field, she's up to bat," Les said morosely.

"What did you tell her?"

Dad answered for him: "That he's in love with Marilyn, infatuated with Crystal, that he hasn't the strength or intelligence for any more involvements, and she should place her affections elsewhere."

I stared at Lester. "You told her *that*?"

"Not in those words."

"What did she *say,* Lester?"

" 'It's a free country; be prepared.' "

I thought again of the 272 awful, ridiculous things that were waiting to happen to me, and wondered whether some might be headed for Lester instead.

Wouldn't it be weird, though, if in spite of all this, Lester grew up to be famous? If, when you looked up the *M*s in the encyclopedia, there was an entry for McKinley, Lester Paul? And if somewhere in his biography there was a listing for Loretta Jenkins, as a girl who knew him when . . . ?

13

In Between

I WAS looking up Madame Curie in the encyclopedia later when there was a thud on the windowpane beside my chair. I looked up to see the slushy remains of a snowball go sliding slowly down the glass, and then Patrick, standing out in the yard, motioning me to come out. I jumped up and went for my boots and jacket.

"Fight?" Patrick said when I stepped outside.

"Fight!" I agreed. As soon as I reached the bottom step, he hit me on the legs, and the war was on.

"Alice, want some help?" Elizabeth called from across the street.

"Sure! Come on!"

It was only fifteen minutes before there was a whole bunch of kids in the street. Elizabeth and I were using the lids of garbage cans for shields, and snowballs were flying like crazy.

"Girls against boys!" someone yelled, and Patrick and Mark Stedmeister and some of the others moved behind a fence a few doors down.

It was snowing harder now, and all of us had frosted eyelashes and tufts of white above our foreheads. The crowd had grown to thirteen, seven boys and six girls. We had scouts on each side who sized up the opposition, spies who crept into no-man's-land, advance troops, rear guards. We agreed to break for supper, then come back later to build a fort.

The crowd was smaller at seven—Elizabeth had gone on to her aunt's for the night, and Mark had to go somewhere with his parents. Only boys showed up, in fact, but we rolled huge balls of snow and made a horseshoe-shaped fort in the middle of our front yard. It was five feet high and had narrow windows so we could see out.

"Al," Dad called from the porch. "Pamela's on the phone and wants to know when you're coming over."

The earring club! The Sisterhood!

"Tell her I can't come tonight, Dad. I'll call her tomorrow," I said, and went on helping to build the last row of the snow fort.

It was there Brian tried to kiss me. Maybe if he had just grabbed me and done it, it wouldn't have been so bad, but it seemed as though wherever I turned, there was Brian, right in my face.

Once I even paused to let him kiss me and get it over with, and he was so close I could smell the wet wool of his cap. But then he lost his nerve and messed up my hair instead. I went to work making another window, and suddenly there was Brian on the other side, looking in.

"Hey, Alice," he said. "Give me an Eskimo kiss." The other guys laughed.

"What?" I said.

"Come on," he said through the narrow window. "An Eskimo kiss." I guess he wanted me to stick my nose in the slot, but at that moment I was very, very sick of Brian. I picked up a clump of snow from the floor of the fort and pushed in through the window, right into Brian's face.

You know what he did? He came around the side, pushed me down, and rubbed my face in the snow, just like I was a boy. The other guys looked embarrassed. Brian's own face was pink. I could see it in the light from the streetlamp. No girl had ever pushed snow in his face before.

"Let's go home," he said to the other guys, and after some more teasing and calling back and forth, they all left, Patrick too.

I went in the house, my cheeks fiery red, my fingers stinging. Why isn't life ever like the movies? Why couldn't Brian have taken me in his arms in front of all the other boys, even Patrick, and kissed me passionately there in the moonlight, with our snow-covered eyelashes beating time with our hearts? Whenever he teased me, I was supposed to laugh. When I teased him, he got mad. It was humiliating.

I sat blowing on my fingers, trying to shake some

life back into them, and Dad mixed a cup of cocoa and gave it to me with a lecture on frostbite.

Lester was over in the corner reading the newspaper, and I remembered his walk in the snow with Loretta, woman of the nineties. I guess for Lester it wasn't like the movies, either. It could have been Marilyn who showed up at the door, and Lester could have proposed under a pine tree or something. But who did he get? Loretta. Does life like to play tricks, or what?

Once I lost the numbness in my fingers and toes, I realized that it was ten o'clock on a Friday night, and I had nothing to do. Lester was in a rotten mood, Dad was finishing up the income tax, Elizabeth was at her aunt's, and the earring club had met without me. Pamela, Jill, and Karen—three of the most popular girls in seventh grade—had tried on earrings and sweaters and eye shadow, and I had said no, I wasn't coming. Once you say no, I discovered, you have to be prepared to spend some evenings by yourself. Was I ready for that? I wasn't sure.

On Saturday, after I'd put in my three hours at the Melody Inn, I discovered the earring club had gone to the mall without me too. And because I wasn't there to buy anything, they didn't invite me over on Sunday to try on what I hadn't bought.

But I was thinking about Loretta. I had talked with her just a little at the Gift Shoppe that morning, and she had a determined look in her eye that made me nervous. She said maybe she didn't have a ghost of a chance with Lester, but she'd never forgive herself if she didn't try, and she wanted me to think of all the things he liked to eat, and to give her a list the following Saturday. I told Lester, and he said if I ever told Loretta anything at all about him I could say good-bye to life. I decided that was pretty definite.

But what if she did win out over Marilyn and Crystal? What if Lester *did* decide that beneath that wild curly hair and those gum-chewing jaws, there was something he just couldn't live without? I'd already decided that if Lester married Marilyn, the wedding would be held in a meadow, with Marilyn in a long cotton dress and everyone playing guitars. If Lester married Crystal, the wedding would be held in a cathedral, with Crystal in a long satin gown and the organ playing Bach. But I knew in my heart that if Lester married Loretta, it would be before a justice of the peace, and the reception would be in the firehouse with everyone dancing the polka.

These three girls were my three older Sisters of the Sisterhood, and I liked them all. I wanted them to be my friends for life. But Lester had to choose.

By Monday, I had decided to give up the All-Stars Fan Club. I felt uncomfortable around Brian, so I told Pamela that there were other things I wanted to do on Wednesdays (namely, *not* go to the fan club), and she said okay.

When we got on the bus, she and Jill sat together, wearing matching pink-and-black earrings that looked like tiny marbles. Those earrings would have looked great on me, I decided with a pang. They were the best-looking earrings that Tiddly Winks had carried yet, and Saturday was the day I *would* have to decide not to go. I slid into the seat with Elizabeth.

"Did you have a good time at your aunt's?" I asked.

"I always do," said Elizabeth. "She has this huge two-thousand-piece jigsaw puzzle, and we worked all evening to make the border. Then we made chocolate fondue."

"What's that?"

"You melt chocolate and cream in a pot, and then you stick little chunks of pineapple and pound cake and orange slices and stuff in it, and eat it off a fork. It's delicious."

I could have been wearing those pink-and-black earrings that looked like marbles, or *I* could have been swirling orange slices in chocolate. I could have been doing anything at all over the weekend except sitting at home. I wasn't out of the earring club, but I wasn't exactly in. I wasn't enemies with Elizabeth, but I wasn't her best friend. I wasn't really Patrick's one true love, either, and I didn't know *what* Brian felt about me. I was just sort of in between everything.

Patrick, Brian, and Mark Stedmeister got on at the next stop. Patrick didn't look too well, I thought. Instead of going to the back with the other guys as he usually does, he just stood there behind the driver, holding on to the pole, looking strange. The bus started up, Patrick took a few steps down the aisle, then stopped again. And suddenly, without any warning, he leaned over and threw up.

Splat! It sounded like a jar full of chili hitting the floor. Elizabeth gave a shriek. A couple of the other girls were screeching too, and somebody said, "Oh, yuk!"

"Way to go, Patrick!" Brian yelled.

"Breakfast, anybody?" called Mark Stedmeister, and laughed.

The awful thing about vomit is, you don't want to look, but you do. I looked down and saw this huge puddle that was running in little rivulets down the aisle. Little bits of undigested Cheerios, little flecks of something orange. Brown specks covered Pamela's white sneakers, and she was frantically wiping at them with a Kleenex.

Patrick started to straighten up, his face white, then leaned over and heaved again.

"Get *off*!" somebody said to Patrick.

"Barf city!" Brian yelled.

The driver stopped the bus.

"You think you ought to go back home?" he said, and Patrick turned and nodded. The door swung open, Patrick escaped, and the driver picked up a copy of the morning *Post* by his seat, unfolded it, and came back to spread the open sheets over the mess on the floor.

You could still smell it, though, and once or twice, I found myself gagging. I didn't want them to, but my eyes kept returning to those newspapers on the floor, knowing what was underneath. And when the bus stopped at last, we all had to step over it to get out. Elizabeth kept one hand over her nose and mouth all the way into the building.

I was thinking of what Lester had told me after I'd

embarrassed myself at the talent show—how everyone else was so glad it happened to me and not to them. I realized I felt some of that now. I was grateful it hadn't happened to me, but I wasn't at all glad it had happened to Patrick.

Things weren't the same in world studies, and it wasn't because of Patrick. Brian wasn't rude to me; he simply didn't pay any attention to me at all. It was as though I'd been quickly, quietly dropped from the Register of Beautiful People. When the bell rang at the end of the period, the others surged out the door, teasing and tickling and laughing their tinkly laughs, but I wasn't one of the Famous Eight. I don't think Pamela even noticed I wasn't along. Maybe none of the others noticed except Brian. Usually, at the end of the period, he herded me over to the door, giving me little pokes in the back and ribs, but on this day, as soon as the bell rang, he was out of there, and I walked through the door by myself.

There were tears in my eyes, and I couldn't help it. If I'd had Carol there right then, or even Aunt Sally, I probably would have buried my head on her bosom and bawled. Was this the price of being popular—one little mistake and you were out? Whose rules were these, anyway? One part of me wanted to plead with Pamela to talk the others into taking me back, and another part of me said that if Brian pushed his face in mine the way he'd done in our yard, he'd get a snout full of snow all over again, and maybe some down his neck for good measure.

14

The Test

LESTER CAME home that evening to say that he just didn't know what to tell Crystal. I decided I didn't want to see Crystal hurt any more than I wanted Marilyn to be hurt, or even Loretta.

"Les," I said to him, "if you're in love with Marilyn, why don't you just tell Crystal you're sorry, but you know she'll be happier with someone else, and then tell Loretta she's not even in the running. Be honest about it."

For once I think I'd said something intelligent, and Lester actually looked as though he were paying attention. But then I had to ruin it: "Crystal could be the maid of honor at your wedding, and Loretta could be a bridesmaid," I said. "Then all three would be happy."

"Get lost, Al," said Lester.

I heard him talking to Dad, though. I was sitting on the edge of my bed, cutting my toenails, and Dad was out in the hall, standing in the doorway of Lester's room.

"If only I was one hundred percent sure about Marilyn," Lester said. "How do you know absolutely, positively, that this is the girl for you?"

"Les, we're never one hundred percent sure of anything in this life," Dad told him. "What you need to help you decide is experience and time. After you've gone with a number of women, you can make a better decision. Don't rush things."

"I've already *gone* with a number, Dad. Counting Josephine Stevens back in fifth grade, I've dated fourteen different girls. How many did you date before you married Mom?"

There was a long silence from the hallway.

"Six," Dad said finally.

"I rest my case," said Lester.

What Dad didn't understand about Lester, though, was that he's never been too good about time. When Lester wants something, he wants it *now*. Still, giving up Crystal entirely so he could devote himself to Marilyn gave him the jitters.

I thought I could help Lester if I could find out how you knew for sure you were in love—from someone who had been there, I mean. If there was a formula or something, wouldn't it help? I obviously couldn't ask Marilyn, Crystal, or Loretta. And if I called Miss Summers and asked how she knew when she was in love,

Dad would kill me. I figured that in a case like this, where Lester might do something desperate, Aunt Sally was better than nothing at all, so I called her long distance.

I told her how Lester and Marilyn were going together again. "He thinks he's in love, Aunt Sally, and I wondered if you knew of any way a person could tell for sure."

"Oh, good grief!" said Aunt Sally. "It's times like this, Alice, that you especially need a mother. I don't know what to tell you. Milt and I just knew, that's all. Once . . . somewhere . . . I read about a test you could take. . . ."

I wondered if it was like a drugstore pregnancy test we'd learned about in Our Changing Bodies. Maybe all Lester had to do was kiss a piece of litmus paper, and if it turned blue, it was negative: He wasn't in love.

"I can almost remember it," said Aunt Sally. "Here's the way it goes, I think: If Lester was stranded out in the desert with Marilyn and the greatest scientist the world had ever known, and the horse could only carry two people, whom would he take with him to go for help: Marilyn or the scientist?"

I stared at the telephone in my hand and wondered if I'd dialed a wrong number. "Huh?" I said.

"It's supposed to help you decide whether you're marrying the right person," Aunt Sally told me.

"What does the scientist have to do with it?"

"I'm not sure exactly, but Lester could probably figure it out."

"If he chooses the scientist, he should marry *him*?"

"Of course not, but then maybe he shouldn't marry Marilyn, either. Actually, Alice, I read this in a magazine at the dentist's, only someone had torn out the answer. And that was a long time ago."

Maybe nobody *was* better than Aunt Sally.

Lester came home late that night, so I didn't get a chance to give him Aunt Sally's test. I was going to try it out on Patrick the next day, but he wasn't at school, so I called him that evening to find out how he was.

"Better, I guess. I only puked twice today."

"I'm really sorry, Patrick," I said. "I know you must feel awful."

"I feel worse about what happened on the bus. I bet everyone was disgusted."

"It could have happened to any of us," I told him.

"What did they say after I got off?"

"Just that they hoped you'd get better," I lied. I didn't tell him about the newspaper on the floor, and the way Pamela kept saying "Yuk" while she wiped her sneakers.

"Listen, Patrick," I said. "You want to take a quiz? It's not about school or anything. But if you and I were stranded out in the desert with the greatest scientist the world had ever known, and the horse could only carry two, who would you pick to go with you for help—me or the scientist?"

The thing I like about Patrick is he never acts like you're nuts.

"What's the matter with the horse?" he asked. "Why did it get lost in the first place?"

"I don't know, but that's not the point," I said. "You're stranded."

"If only two people can ride it, how did they all get out there to begin with?" he wanted to know.

"That's not the *point*, Patrick! The point is you have to make a choice between me and the greatest scientist the world has ever known. Which will it be?"

"Wait a minute. I think I'm going to throw up again," he said, and I heard the receiver clunk down on his dresser, the thud of feet against the floor, then the sound of somebody heaving. The corners of my mouth began to twitch.

"Listen," I said when he came back, "I'll call you tomorrow."

"No, it's okay. I'm bored. About this quiz, is someone in it supposed to die?"

"I don't know. Whoever you leave behind, I suppose."

"Then maybe I could save you both. Two people ride while one person walks, and then that person rides while someone else walks, and—"

"Patrick, just forget the horse, okay? If you had to make a choice between me and the greatest scientist the world had ever known—"

"Wait a minute, Alice, I've got the runs now," he said.

"I'll call you tomorrow, Patrick," I told him, and hung up.

At dinner, I could tell that Lester was still thinking of Marilyn, because he sat with one sleeve in the applesauce. Dad was working overtime, so it was just Les and me.

"Lester," I said, "here's a little test to help you decide whether or not you're truly in love."

"Yeah?"

"If you were stranded in the desert with Marilyn and the greatest scientist the world had ever known, and your horse would only carry two, who would you choose to ride with you when you went for help— Marilyn or the scientist?"

"We used to argue about things like that back in Scouts," said Lester.

"Well, who would you choose?" I asked.

"That's supposed to show the difference between selfish love and love for mankind, Al. If I go off and leave Marilyn to die, see, I'm the one who would suffer most. But if I leave the great scientist to die, then all humanity would be the losers. The fact is, if I'm so noble, why wouldn't I put Marilyn and the scientist both on the horse, and stay behind *myself?*"

I was beginning to feel hopeless. "I don't know, but maybe you're the only one who could find the way back."

"He's the greatest scientist the world has ever known, and *I'm* leading the way?" Lester said.

But I wasn't through yet, because when Marilyn called Lester that evening, I was the one who answered. And before I called Les to the phone, I said,

"Marilyn, I've got this little quiz. If you were stranded on the desert with Lester and the greatest scientist the world had ever known, and the horse would only carry two people, who would you choose to go with you for help—Lester or the scientist?"

There was absolute silence from the other end of the line.

"How old is the scientist?" Marilyn asked finally.

"I don't know."

"Is he married?"

"That's not the point!" I said.

"It would depend on what had been happening between Les and me, Alice. If things were going well, I'd take Les, of course, but if he'd even *looked* at Crystal Harkins lately, then . . ."

I decided that the next time Aunt Sally had a quiz, I'd be two miles out the door. I don't think she knows any more about love than I do, and that's not very much.

You know what I wish? That when it's my turn to fall in love, Elizabeth and Pamela and I—all the girls in the seventh grade, in fact—would all fall in love at the same time, like graduation, or something. And that if anyone gives me a Vivaldi cassette when I'm expecting a ring, or balloons when I'm not expecting anything at all, I'll know exactly what to do.

15

All but Alice

SOMETIMES DAD and Lester and I have a quiet night at home, and sometimes it's *very* quiet. That night was in the "very" category.

Dad must have finished the income tax, because the papers that had been spread out over the dining-room table for six weeks had been placed in neat piles, with bunches clipped together here and there, and stacks of canceled checks neatly held together with rubber bands.

In the past, when he's through with a job he doesn't like, such as cleaning the oven, he usually plays the piano—something strenuous, that takes a lot of arm movement and fingering, something fast and loud and rhythmical. But on this night he got out his flute and played slow, soft melodies—not really happy, not really sad—what I call Question Mark Music, because you can't tell for sure what the composer was thinking. He only played for a short while. Then he poured himself a glass of wine and sat sipping it slowly, staring somewhere up on the wall between the pictures and the ceiling.

It was quiet upstairs too. The reason Dad doesn't play the stereo more downstairs is that Les is usually playing CDs so loud upstairs. But tonight there wasn't any sound at all from Lester's room except for the soft chewing of Fritos whenever I passed his door. I noticed that on the calendar above our phone, on the Saturday square, Lester had written, "Dinner with Marilyn," then erased it, then penciled it in again, crossed it out, then tried to erase the cross mark. So Saturday night was anybody's guess.

I had only two more days to do the assignment for Hensley, and I wasn't getting very far with that. I wasn't getting very far with my friends, either. Being one of the Beautiful People had only got me a face full of snow. I wanted someone to cuddle up to, and the first person who came to mind was my sixth-grade teacher, which was strange, because I've never cuddled up to her once, except for the time I'd hugged her when she gave me her ring.

I walked across the bedroom and took it down from the bulletin board. Mrs. Plotkin's great-grandmother had given it to her. It had a large green stone that made it top-heavy, so that it rolled around on my finger and faced the wrong way. She didn't have any children of her own and had wanted to pass it on.

If someone likes you enough to give you her ring,

I decided, she wouldn't mind if you called once in a while. So before I could think of all the reasons not to, I looked up her number, dragged the extension phone in my bedroom, and dialed.

A man answered, and I had to remind myself that she was married. Somebody else had loved that large pear-shaped woman as much as I did.

"Hello, Plotkin residence," the man said. It was a nice voice, a radio announcer's voice.

"Is Mrs. Plotkin home?" I asked, hating the way my voice squeaked.

"She's out visiting a friend. Is there a message?"

"No," I told him. "I'll call some other time." And I hung up.

So much for the cuddle. And yet I felt better just having dialed her number—as though it had connected me to something important. I couldn't figure out what it was. Mrs. Plotkin didn't dress as nicely as the other teachers. Nobody would say she was exciting, exactly. And yet . . .

Alice, how nice to hear your voice! How are you? I was sure she would have said that. I could almost *hear* her saying it.

Fine. I could hear *me* saying *that.* Fine, meaning lousy.

I had my ears pierced. I'd probably tell her that too.

Did you, dear? What kind of earrings are you wearing? Tell me about it.

And I would tell her about that and about the

Three Handsome Stooges, and how I was going to drop out of the earring club because it was boring. I blinked. I was?

That seems wise, Alice, Mrs. Plotkin would say. Thinking about it was almost as good as talking to her directly. And then I heard her telling me that I was the daughter she'd never had, and her most favorite pupil, and that she and her husband wanted to adopt me every summer and introduce me to all her relatives and take me on a trip to Spain, and about that moment the real world kicked back in.

It was the next morning on my way to the bus stop that I got the answer about the common characteristics of great men and women—*my* answer, anyway: There weren't any. They were all different, and they didn't care. Like Mrs. Plotkin, maybe.

Pamela and Elizabeth were already at the corner with some of the other kids, and they both spoke to me so I guessed I wasn't a total wipeout. We were still friends, like we'd promised we'd be forever that summer between sixth and seventh grades.

And then, wonder of wonders, I saw Brian and one of the other Stooges running down the block toward us, and Brian was smiling and calling my name. *He* obviously wasn't mad at me, either. We'd pushed snow in each other's faces and were still friends. There *was* life after all the mistakes of seventh grade.

I wondered why the boys had come down to our stop. They usually got on at Patrick's.

"Alice," Brian said, "how'd you like to go onstage?"

"Huh?" I said. "You must be joking."

Another boy came running up, and Brian gathered us all into a huddle, one arm around me, the other around Pamela.

"Listen," he said. "Patrick's coming back to school today. He told Mark. We're going to pull something on him. As soon as he gets on, I want all you girls to scream, like he's going to upchuck on you again. Mark's going to sit behind the girls, and after they scream, he's going to gag and clutch his throat. Here's where you come in, Alice. You'll be sitting behind Mark, and we want you to pull that little routine you do in Hensley's class sometimes—lean over the aisle and pretend to barf. Really pour it on. And then I'll stand up at the back, take a few steps forward, open my mouth, and release this. . . ." He disentangled himself from the group, reached in his jacket pocket, and pulled out a little plastic Ziploc bag filled with a half cup of water and some Cheerios.

"Ooh!" the girls said, and giggled.

Brian grinned. "All over the floor, right at Patrick's feet. It'll be a scream."

My mouth was smiling, but I think my tongue was frozen to my tonsils or something. I knew how Patrick felt about what had happened on the bus—how embarrassed *any*one would have been. Still, Patrick could take a joke. I mean, Patrick's been all around the world. He can hold his own in any class discussion. He'd probably laugh himself. Here was my chance to redeem myself from the talent show, get back my membership in the Famous Eight, and do something really hilarious. Funny Girl, just like my mom. Maybe I couldn't sing or dance, but I could barf like nobody's business, and it would be a scream.

The bus was coming up the street.

"Okay, you got it, now?" Brian said, looking around. "Patrick gets on, you girls start to scream, Mark gags, Alice does her barf routine, and then I'll unload the Cheerios."

Everyone giggled.

I climbed inside the bus and sat where Brian told me. Pamela and Elizabeth were sitting in front with the other girls. All the boys were grinning.

We rode for a couple of blocks, and then we could see Patrick standing on the corner with some other kids—his jacket unzipped, books under his arm, hands in his pockets, hunched against the wind.

"As soon as he gets on," Brian stage-whispered.

My heart was beating double time like it did backstage at the talent show. As the door of the bus swung open, it was my cue, as though I could hear the music to *Guys and Dolls*. Patrick was the first one on, and the girls up front all screamed dramatically and pulled away from him. Patrick stared and instantly his face reddened. I remembered the way my face had burned at the talent show.

It was Mark's turn now, and he clutched his throat and started to gag.

And then: "Hey, Patrick," a voice said. It was mine. "Sit here. I've got something to tell you."

"Aww," came a disappointed chorus from the other kids. Faces turned and looked at me in disgust. Patrick slid gratefully onto the seat beside me, and behind us came the sound of someone spitting a mouthful of water into a Ziploc bag.

"Spoilsport," I heard Brian mutter as he leaned over the seats and punched my shoulder. Hard. I didn't even turn around.

"What is it?" Patrick asked as the bus pulled away again. "What'd you want to tell me?"

My mind searched desperately for ideas. "Do you know the story of Gounod's 'Ave Maria'?" I asked.

"What?" asked Patrick, staring.

"Well, Gounod wrote this music, see, and someone figured out that it would go well with one of Bach's preludes, and . . ."

"What are you talking about?"

I went on explaining the story of how "Ave Maria" got mixed up in the mess.

"This is what you wanted to tell me?"

I nodded.

"You're weird sometimes, Alice," Patrick said.

"I know," I answered. But I didn't tell him I was saving his life. I didn't say that if it wasn't for me, he'd have relived that horrible moment on the bus last Monday. I didn't get my name in the hall of fame, exactly, and I was struck forever from the Famous Eight, but I was glad I'd rescued Patrick.

"Remember that problem about being stranded on the desert?" Patrick said. "I've been thinking about it some more, and I guess I'd choose you, because I figure the greatest scientist who ever lived could find his own way back. I know you couldn't."

"Thanks, Patrick," I said.

I liked sitting beside him on the bus. There was a warm spot where our thighs were touching. We weren't cuddling, but it was the next best thing, I guess. There was something nice about being Patrick's "special friend," as he called it, and I wanted him to know that.

"Patrick," I said, "remember that valentine you sent me in sixth grade?" I'd hardly finished the sentence when I saw the color creeping up in his face. Maybe he remembered the envelope with the drawings of hearts and airplanes too. But I hadn't meant to embarrass him. "Well," I went on, "I've still got it. And know what else? The wrapper off that Three Musketeers bar, and the matches from the country club."

Patrick looked at me strangely. "Why?"

I shrugged. "Because they're special to me, I guess."

You know what Patrick did? He reached over, grabbed my shoulders, and kissed me on the mouth. In front of the other boys at the back. It wasn't a kiss in the moonlight with our snow-covered eyelashes beating time with our hearts; it was a kiss in the school bus with the smell and taste of orange juice on Patrick's lips.

Brian started yelling like a baboon and the boys all stomped their feet on the floor, which made all the kids in front turn around. And you know what happened next? Patrick kissed me again. When a seventh-grade boy can't think of anything else to do, he kisses.

As we went inside the school, Elizabeth said, "I'm glad you didn't play that trick on Patrick. I never saw his face get that red, Alice. I wish I hadn't been one of the ones to scream."

Brian wasn't so kind. "You're a killjoy, you know it?" he told me. "All the other kids did their part. All but you. It would have been a blast!"

"For you, maybe," I said.

It was Pamela who surprised me, though. As we walked to our lockers, she said, "You and Elizabeth and Patrick and I have known each other since sixth grade, Alice. I think you did exactly the right thing."

I did? You mean there was a Brotherhood too? Or maybe a Universal Humanhood that included Brian and Dad and Lester and even Mr. Hensley? Who came first? My family? My friends? Myself? The Sisters? Or did you have to decide it case by case? It was all very confusing. The important thing, however, was that Pamela and Elizabeth and I were Sisters again. Friends forever, just as we'd promised.

At lunchtime, however, I told Jill and Karen that I didn't want to come to the earring club any longer, because I was saving my money for something else. They didn't seem too surprised.

"What are you saving for?" Pamela asked me.

I had to think quickly. "A dress," I said, and that seemed to satisfy them.

And maybe it *would* be a dress, who knows? A bridesmaid's dress for whoever got married first, Lester or Dad. Would Lester marry Marilyn? Would Crystal find another love? Would Loretta get lost? Would Janice Sherman walk down the aisle with the oboe instructor? Would Dad marry Miss Summers? The only thing I knew for sure was that nothing stays the same, and whatever was coming next, I'd be ready. Maybe.